Hotel Paradiso

A FARCE-COMEDY IN THREE ACTS

by

Georges Feydeau and Maurice Desvallieres

English Translation by
PETER GLENVILLE

SAMUEL FRENCH, INC.

45 WEST 25TH STREET   NEW YORK 10010
7623 SUNSET BOULEVARD HOLLYWOOD 90046
LONDON   TORONTO

HOTEL PARADISO

STORY OF THE PLAY

(13 males; 8 females; extras)

This "mad French bedroom frolic" (*N. Y. Journal-American*) finds an assortment of refined people stealing through the halls and rooms of a cheap hotel comically intent on assignations. There is the hero, the henpecked husband, who arrives in disguise with his friend's wife; a tottering octogenarian and a chorus girl; a stiff youth on his first flight with a housemaid; a housing inspector investigating ghosts; a nosey bellboy who impales our hero with a brace and bit as he bores through the wall for a peek, and a host of others, including the police who raid the joint at the second act curtain.

HOTEL PARADISO

Farce in three acts by Georges Feydeau and Maurice Desvallieres, adapted and staged by Peter Glenville; settings and costumes by Osbert Lancaster; supervised by Charles Lisanby and produced by arrangement with Hardy W. Smith and H. M. Tennent, Ltd.; associate producer Will Lester Productions; presented by Richard Myers, Julius Fleischman, Charles Bowden, Richard Barr and H. Ridgely Bullock, Jr., at Henry Miller's Theatre, April 11, 1957.

THE CAST

BONIFACE	_Bert Lahr_
ANGELIQUE	_Vera Pearce_
MARCELLE	_Angela Lansbury_
COT	_John Emery_
MAXIME	_Carleton Carpenter_
VICTOIRE	_Sondra Lee_
MARTIN	_Douglas Byng_
1ST PORTER	_Neil Laurence_
2ND PORTER	_Mark Lang_
3RD PORTER	_Fred Baker_
4TH PORTER	_Roy Johnson_
VIOLETTE	_Joan-Ellen Caine_
MARGUERITE	_Nancy Devlin_
PAQUERETTE	_Patricia Fay_
PERVENCHE	_Helen Quarter_
ANNIELLO	_Ronald Radd_
GEORGES	_James Bernard_
A LADY	_Lucille Benson_
A DUKE	_Horace Cooper_
TABU	_James Coco_
POLICE INSPECTOR	_George Tyne_

SCENES

Hotel Paradiso

ACT ONE

*Period 1910. The home of M. and Mme. Boniface, in
Passy. A builder's room. Upstage back Center a
large window with iron bar on the outside. Trees
can be seen from window. To the Left, downstage,
door to Mme. Boniface's bedroom. Up Left is a door
opening on corridor or landing. Door Right to M.
Boniface's bedroom. In back Center, near window
but far enough to permit passage, a large drawing
board on trestles. On this, papers and other architect's materials, plus a telephone directory. At this
table, a high stool. Between steps and Boniface's
room a commode with doors, with samples of tiles,
stones, etc. On Right, between footlights and door,
a large desk against wall on which are plans and
drawings in rolls, books, etc. Above this desk a
mirror, Downstage, Right Center, a sofa. At Left,
between wall and steps, a desk [secretaire style].
The window is closed.*

(The CURTAIN RISES *on an empty stage.)*

*(*BONIFACE, *a nervous meticulous little man in middle
years, enters from his bedroom Right, picks up
pencil and pen-knife from his desk Right, and walks
to the footlights sharpening his pencil, and singing.)*

BONIFACE. *(Crosses to desk Up Left.)*
    Oh, Spring, give your fragrance of roses—
*(Suddenly sees the audience, crosses up to trestle table
and says:)* Aah!
    ANGELIQUE. *(Off-stage.)* Boniface!

7

BONIFACE. (*Looking at audience.*) Later. (*Moving up to trestle table and sitting with his back to the audience, starts to sing again.*)
Oh, Spring, give your fragrance of roses,
Oh, Spring, give your gleam of the sun.

(ANGELIQUE [*Mme. Boniface*] *enters Left, trailing two long lengths of material after her. She is a large, formidable woman with a bellicose manner.*)

ANGELIQUE. (*To Down Right front of sofa.*) Boniface!—Boniface!
BONIFACE. (*Without turning.*) Angelique?
ANGELIQUE. The dressmaker is here!
BONIFACE. Good—good— Tra-la!—la!—la!—la! (*He goes on working.*)
ANGELIQUE. Kindly stop working when I talk to you!
BONIFACE. (*Working.*) Tum-ti-tum—tedious tum—tedious, tedious,, tedious *tum!* (*Swivelling around to her.*) My pet, I am trying to solve a very tricky problem. This house——
ANGELIQUE. The house can wait!
BONIFACE. (*Patiently.*) As you please, my sweet! (*Comes Downstage.*)
ANGELIQUE. (*Right end of sofa; displaying the samples.*) Now! I can't make up my mind between these two materials. Which would you choose?
BONIFACE. It's for a sofa?
ANGELIQUE. Certainly not! It's for me!
BONIFACE. (*Fingering one.*) I prefer this one.
ANGELIQUE. Thank you, my dear. I'll have the other! (*Picks up material.*)
BONIFACE. Then why ask *me*, my sweet?
ANGELIQUE. Because you have no taste whatsoever. (*Crosses Left.*) Now I know which one I can throw out! (*Stops at Left door.*) Now get on with your work! (*She rolls up materials and papers and sweeps out.*)
BONIFACE. (*Up to table; with soft surprise, to the*

audience.) And I married for love!— I really did! And
my whole family were against it! (*He shakes his head
and turns away, back to work. Musing; comes Down
Center*.) Oh the ladies—if only one could picture them
twenty years later—how cautious one would be twenty
years earlier. I was a fool! (*Crosses up and looks toward
the window*.) Tt—tt—tt— It looks threatening— (*To
desk Right and picks up T square*.) Mark my words,
we'll have rain— My son will never marry against my
will— (*Pause*.) But then I haven't got a son—and I
don't intend to have one— (*Singing; crosses Left to
above sofa*.) Never—never—never—never.
    (*He works. There is a* KNOCK.)
Come in!

(MARCELLE [*Mme. Cot*] *enters. A pretty and panicky
    woman of thirty-nine, in a dressing-gown. He hurries
    towards her to Left end of sofa*.)

MARCELLE. (*Rather anguished, in a scatter-brained
way*.) Good afternoon, M. Boniface. Forgive my being
dressed like this.
    BONIFACE. (*Warmly*.) Aha—*dear* Mme. Cot! It's the
privilege of old friends with adjoining villas.
    MARCELLE. That's what I said to myself. Is your wife
at home?
    BONIFACE. (*Crosses to* MARCELLE.) Yes. In conference
with her dressmaker. How is your husband?
    MARCELLE. I have no idea! (*She turns away*.)
    BONIFACE. (*Taking her hands and looking into her
eyes*.) Something's the matter?
    MARCELLE. Nothing!
    BONIFACE. Yes, it is. It is! You have pink eyes!
    MARCELLE. No, no. It's nothing. Really—nothing,
nothing at all!
    BONIFACE. Pink eyes.
    MARCELLE. Oh, well— (*She sniffs, crosses Right and
upstage*.) Just the usual thing—another scene.

BONIFACE. You poor, poor thing! (*He pats her hands.*) Has he been a brute? Has he been a beast?

MARCELLE. If only he would be. That's just the trouble— I'm no more to him than an old shoe. (*She blows her little nose.*) Never mind— I just get myself worked up— (*To Right end of sofa.*) it's silly!— I must have a word with Mme. Boniface. (*Crosses Left front of sofa to door Left.*)

BONIFACE. (*Calling after her.*) And I shall give your husband quite a piece of my mind.

MARCELLE. Oh, don't bother. He wouldn't know chalk from cheese! (*She gives him an anguished look, and exits.*)

BONIFACE. (*Putting on his pince-nez and gazing at the closing door.*) What a woman! Splendid creature! Oh, la, la! (*He crosses up to trestle table; arranges his instruments.*) Splendid creature!— (*Tidying.*) Spleni—spleni —splendid! (*Puts down T square and picks up plans.*) And married to a nincompoop!—A nincompoop!—I should know. He's my best friend! Ah!—if only he weren't! (*Change of tone.*) But then I'm not sure what she thinks of me. I might be rebuffed!— And I'm the last man in the world to want to betray my best friend— especially if it wasn't going to work! (*He hums and unrolls the drawings.*) What on earth has he written down here? (*Crosses down to Right of sofa; comparing it with his own drawings.*) Sandstone! To hold up that *massive weight?*— Cot must be out of his mind— It's always the same with these architects. No sense of durability. (*Moving upstage—change of tone.*) But one must admit he has a splendid wife! Mm! Splendid!

(COT *enters Up Left. A large, important man, with a large beard.*)

COT. (*At door.*) Good afternoon to you, Boniface. Not intruding, I trust?

BONIFACE. No—no—on the contrary. Glad to see you.

What on earth have you put down here? (*Moves to desk down Right.*)

COT. (*Slowly, with an eyebrow raised.*) To what, exactly, do you refer? (*Moves leisurely to Left of* BONIFACE.)

BONIFACE. (*With the passion of an artist.*) You want me to use sandstone for that building? But you're mad!

COT. (*Pauses, then steadily; moving Right below sofa.*) Use what you damn well like as long as it holds together! (*He takes out a cigarette.*) Is my wife here? (*Sits sofa.*)

BONIFACE. (*Moves above sofa Left of* COT.) Yes. In there with Mme. Boniface. And—what have you been doing to her?

COT. Why? Is she fussing again?

BONIFACE. You have only to look in her eyes—they're pink!

COT. (*Very offhand.*) Oh, she's so unreasonable. (*Moves to Left.*) She should be perfectly happy with me— I am faithful— My conduct is beyond reproach— There's no other woman.

BONIFACE. (*Center.*) I should hope not!

COT. Well, what more does she want? She says I'm unresponsive!

BONIFACE. Oh-hoh-hoh! And are you? (*Over to sofa— sits Left end of sofa.*)

COT. My dear Boniface, one can't be responsive with one's own wife— Damn it, sir, are you always so responsive with yours?

BONIFACE. My dear Cot— Consider the lady!— And after twenty years one must call a halt!

COT. Mine always expects a forward march! (*Crosses his legs and studies* BONIFACE.) Well, why don't you have a little adventure on the side? (*Lights cigarette.*)

BONIFACE. (*Shocked.*) Oh, really! What a thing to suggest—you! The faithful husband!

COT. Oh, my dear fellow, that's different. I'm kept busy all day, climbing scaffoldings, crawling under floors— I come home exhausted and go early to bed and *sleep like a top!*— That's what my wife complains of!— She says it shows lack of respect!

BONIFACE. (*To front.*) To say the least!

COT. Well, there you are! I'm no Don Juan—never have been. That's why I married. I lack the temperament.

BONIFACE. In other words, you're a great big whiskered iceberg!

COT. Iceberg! Well, Boniface, I wouldn't describe you as piping hot!

BONIFACE. (*Rises and backs up to Up Left corner of sofa.*) Let me tell you, Cot, that deep down inside (*He taps a fragile chest.*) I'm seething with molten lava!—

COT. Molten lava!— You—a volcano! (*Rises and goes Right to Up Right end of sofa.*) Don't make me laugh!— Incidentally, could I borrow your maid?

BONIFACE. (*Alarmed.*) Borrow? Whatever for?

COT. Max—my nephew.

BONIFACE. For Max?

COT. Oh, don't be alarmed— The poor boy (*Crosses away Left to Left Center.*) is far too serious for that sort of thing. He thinks of nothing but philosophy.

BONIFACE. Poor boy!

COT. (*Goes Down Left Center.*) Anyway, he goes back tonight to his school at Stanislaus—and you know what he is—with his head in the clouds—he'll never get on the right trains unless somebody goes with him—the wife's in hysterics—

BONIFACE. (*To Right of* COT.) Of course— I'll arrange it. But why can't you take him back yourself?

COT. No time! Every minute completely booked up!— Even this evening— I'll have to stay up in town tonight!

BONIFACE. Oho! (*Digs him in the ribs.*)

COT. Entirely on my own, I assure you.

BONIFACE. Indeed!

COT. Certainly, my dear sir. I have to spend the night

in some beastly little hotel— They say it's haunted by ghosts who make noises during the night.

BONIFACE. Noises during the night! Faulty construction!

COT. Exactly. I'm convinced it comes from the drains!

BONIFACE. Of course!

COT. The point is, the tenant wants to break his lease because of the ghosts, and the owner won't agree. So the court has appointed me, as an expert, to arbitrate. So I have to spend the night there, and see for myself—

BONIFACE. That the ghosts are escaping bath water?

COT. Precisely! (*He moves to go.*)

BONIFACE. (*Moves Right.*) And what does your wife think of *that?*

COT. Oh, I've had one scene after another this morning. She says I take every opportunity to leave her on her own. I tried to make her understand that my work as an architect comes first. (*Crosses to door Up Left.*)

BONIFACE. (*Crosses to Left end of sofa.*) Be careful that as a man you don't come second!

COT. What do you mean?

BONIFACE. Well, you'd have no one but yourself to blame!

COT. What do you mean!

BONIFACE. (*Crosses to* COT.) Well— I should hate to see it happen.

COT. What?

BONIFACE. If your wife took it into her head to replace you—

COT. (*Dismissing the idea with a laugh; crosses Right a bit.*) Replace me!— My wife! My dear sir, with whom?

BONIFACE. Very well, go your own way.

COT. I certainly shall.

(*There is a* KNOCK.)

BONIFACE. Come in!

(MAXIME *enters Up Left with a book under his arm. He is a lanky, earnest youth, with thick-lensed glasses.*)

COT. Oh, it's you, Max.

MAX. Yes, Uncle. I hope I'm not intruding. (*Crosses up to trestle table.*)

BONIFACE. No. Not at all.

COT. What's the trouble?

MAX. I don't know where my Payne has got to— I had it last time I was in here—it's a brand new one.

BONIFACE. (*Hurrying to* MAX.) Pain? Oh, my dear boy, where do you feel it? (*He takes his hand.*)

MAX. No, no, M'sieu. Robert Payne—the writer—the philosopher. (*Crosses down a bit Center.*) It's an essay refuting some of Spinoza's opinions—whose treatise on Passion I'm working on at the moment. (*Indicating a volume.*)

COT. (*Crosses over toward* MAX—*takes book.*) So that's a treatice on Passion.

BONIFACE. (*Crosses toward* MAX.) The theory *and* practice, I hope.

MAX. (*Taking book from* COT.) Certainly not, M'sieu! (*Up to Right of trestle table and searches for book.*)

COT. (*Goes and sits desk chair Up Left.*) Now don't go putting ideas into the boy's head.

BONIFACE. Perfectly natural question. After all, when one learns to play billiards one doesn't just learn the rules, but all the maneuvers.

(VICTOIRE *enters Left. A saucy, good-natured girl in full bloom.*)

VICTOIRE. (*In to Down Left.*) M'sieu!

BONIFACE. What is it?

VICTOIRE. Madame wants you—she's in the middle of her fitting and wants your advice—and have you got a tape measure?

(MAX *above trestle table.*)

BONIFACE. (*Crosses to desk Right.*) Oh dear! Oh dear! Oh dear!

COT. (*To* MAX, *who is rummaging at fire box.*) What on earth are you doing?

MAX. Looking for my philosophy, Uncle!

BONIFACE. Well, you won't find it there, my boy. That's the fire apparatus. Tape measure— You really mustn't go rummaging in my things like that— Victoire, you haven't seen an essay on philosophy by Robert Aches, have you?

VICTOIRE. Aches?

MAX. (*To high stool and sits.*) Robert Payne, M. Boniface!

BONIFACE. Aches— Payne—it's all part of the same thing!

VICTOIRE. I haven't seen it, M'sieu.

MAX. (*Glumly.*) I shall have to buy another one.

BONIFACE. (*Moves up.*) Oh, and Victoire, you will accompany Master Max to college this evening. (*Starts Down Right.*)

VICTOIRE. (*Bright-eyed.*) What fun!

BONIFACE. (*Stops and turns.*) Fun or no fun, you will please to do it! (*Crosses to desk Down Right. To* COT.) What time should he be there?

MAX. By nine o'clock, M. Boniface.

BONIFACE. (*Up Right end sofa.*) Nine o'clock. Is that clear, Victoire?

VICTOIRE. Oh yes, M'sieu! (*She moves to table to tidy some papers.*)

COT. (*Rising, to* BONIFACE.) It's very kind of you, old boy.

BONIFACE. Nothing! Nothing at all!

(MAX *begins to read.*)

ANGELIQUE. (*Offstage.*) Boniface!

BONIFACE. There we go! (*Crosses to door Down Left. Answering.*) Yes, yes, my sweet! Come along, Cot. (*He pushes him.*) You're an architect. Come and give a hand with the wife's fitting!

COT. A great privilege! After you!

BONIFACE. No, after you! I want you to be the first to see the front elevation.

(*They exit.*)

MAX. (*Sitting on high stool, reading.*) "Passion is an emotion of the soul, moved by the impulses of one's animal nature, impelling one to consort with objects that appear suitable." (*Deeply convinced.*) That's exactly it!

VICTOIRE. Exactly what, Master Max?

MAX. I beg your pardon?

VICTOIRE. What are you doing there?

MAX. Studying Passion.

VICTOIRE. (*Skeptical—moves to Left of* MAX *and leans on trestle table.*) Really! In that position? (*Moving towards him.*) If you like I'll help you with your work.

MAX. (*Earnest.*) Have you studied the centres of emotional life?

VICTOIRE. (*Naturally.*) Same as most people!

MAX. In Spinoza?

VICTOIRE. No, in the palm of my hand. (*Moves to Left of trestle table.*)

MAX. I'm afraid you don't quite understand.

VICTOIRE. (*Tickles his ear with quill.*) Are you sure I can't help you with your work?

MAX. (*Imperturbable.*) That tickles.

VICTOIRE. Don't you like it?

MAX. I didn't comment on the nature of the sensation. I stated a fact. It tickles. (*Aside, as he swivels around on the stool.*) What a curious girl!

VICTOIRE. You're not very friendly, are you?

MAX. I am working! (*Gets up.*) I cannot study Passion with a woman next to me! (*He moves to sofa, sits.*

Reading aloud.) "There is a distinction between idealistic love and sensual love. The passion of a lover for his mistress and that of a kind father for his children.

(*VICTOIRE crosses to him above sofa.*)

They have certain emotional impulses in common, but—

(*He looks at VICTOIRE and moves to the other end of the sofa. She sits Left of MAX.*)

—in the first case love is aimed at the *possession* of the object rather than the object itself."

(*She tickles his leg.*)

(*Looking up.*) That is a distinctly pleasant sensation!

VICTOIRE. (*Behind him, coiling a lock of his hair round her finger.*) Think so?

MAX. Undoubtedly! (*Reading.*) "A father seeks the well-being of his children—"

VICTOIRE. (*Up to MAX's shoulder.*) You're a big, big, beautiful baby. (*She continues to play with his hair.*)

MAX. Please, M'selle! You may tickle but don't talk.

VICTOIRE. Yes, M. Max.

MAX. A father seeks the well-being of his children—

VICTOIRE. (*She leans over sofa.*) Has anyone ever told you you're quite a good looker? (*She tickles.*)

MAX. Me? I've no idea. Oh, yes. Once.

VICTOIRE. Who?

MAX. A photographer. He advised me to order three dozen copies.

VICTOIRE. Oh!

MAX. (*Continuing to read.*) "A father seeks the well-being of his children—" (*He pauses. His eyes are raised furtively.*)

VICTOIRE. (*Finger on MAX's knee.*) What is it, M. Max?

MAX. Nothing! Nothing at all! It's just that—well, in some perplexing way—that movement of the hand—it was rather agreeable. I can't think why!

VICTOIRE. Really?— Why not ask Spinoza? (*Takes hand away.*)

MAX. He is silent on the subject!

VICTOIRE. Well, then, I'd shut that silly old book if I were you. (*She takes book and shuts it; gets up, crosses above sofa Left of* MAX.) How can a young man find out about passion in a book! Like learning to swim on a cushion! No good if you're tossed in the sea. (*She sits down beside him.*)

MAX. (*To front.*) What is the matter with this girl?

VICTOIRE. (*Hands on his shoulders.*) Look at you. (*Left of* MAX.) Those awful glasses. (*She takes them off.*) Can't you see without them?

MAX. Oh yes!— In fact, rather better!

VICTOIRE. (*Going behind sofa.*) And just look at your hair! You ought to try a different style. You've got to give nature a helping hand, you know! (*Rumples hair.*)

MAX. (*Closing his eyes, with concentration.*) Do that again!

(*She rumples hair again.*)

Again. Oh yes.

(*Her hands to ears, to chin and down front of chest.*)

That's very, very good! Oh yes, indeed! (*Breaks and grabs book from Left end of sofa.*) "Passion is an emotion of the soul—"

VICTOIRE. M. Maxime.

MAX. Au revoir, M'selle.

VICTOIRE. Au revoir!

MAX. M'selle?

VICTOIRE. (*Goes to the door Up Left.*) It's unbelievable! It's like getting blood from a stone. (*Exits.*)

MAX. (*Reading.*) "The affection of honourable men—"

(*There is a sound of raised* VOICES *off stage.*)

(*Covers his ears with his hands and goes on reading.*) "The affection of honourable men for their friends is in the following category—"

(MARCELLE *enters Left, followed by* COT, BONIFACE *and* ANGELIQUE.)

MARCELLE. (*Crosses Down Right front of sofa. Exasperated.*) No! This is too much!

COT. (*Crosses Center.*) Once and for all, what is the matter with you, woman?

ANGELIQUE. (*Crosses below* COT.) Don't take the slightest notice of him!

MARCELLE. (*Crosses up end of sofa.*) You're making my life insupportable!

ANGELIQUE. Oh my dear, wait till you've been married twenty years, as I have!

BONIFACE. (*Crosses to Right of* COT.) What are you going on about? For twenty years I've done everything humanly possible to make you happy.

COT. And so have I! She can't deny it!

ANGELIQUE *and* MARCELLE. Happy! Ha! Ha! Ha! I like that!

(MARCELLE *above* ANGELIQUE *to Left.*)

BONIFACE *and* COT. Yes, you know you're happy!

WOMEN. Happy! Ha! Ha! Ha! Ha!

COT. Laugh away.

BONIFACE. Laugh away!

COT. You've been happy for years.

BONIFACE. You've been happy for years!

ALL FOUR. Yes! No! Yes! How dare you?— (*Etc.*)

MAX. (*Rising.*) Stop! Stop! How can one be expected to work? This is Bedlam! (*He leaves Up Left as they continue to argue.*)

MARCELLE. (*Crosses Down Right below sofa.*) Why did I ever marry him? For *what?*—I ask you!

COT. (*Center.*) Really, Marcelle!— Not in front of the neighbors—

MARCELLE. He thinks I married him to look after his house— (*Sits on sofa.*) That's all I am—a glorified cook-general! He ignores me—he doesn't know I'm there—I'm left—abandoned—it's tantamount to desertion.

Cot. No, no! Now you really are exaggerating! (*Crosses up.*)

Angelique. Desertion! (*Crosses above sofa to* Marcelle.) Oh, my dear, that must be terrible for you. Boniface and I have been together for twenty years (*Crosses Up Center.*) but if ever he behaved like that to me— Oh, ho, ho, ho! We'd soon see! (*She crosses to above Right of* Boniface, *rolls her eyes and smiles complacently.*)

Cot. (*To his wife.*) Well, what the devil do you want? Do you expect me to stay in tonight and give up this important survey?

Marcelle. No! Go to your beastly old pipes and drains. Whether you're in or out, it makes no difference—the amount of attention you pay to me!

Cot. (*Crosses below sofa to desk Down Right.*) Oh, the old refrain!

Marcelle. Do you think I'd have married you if I'd known what it would be like? I think it's a miracle that I've never looked at another man!

Cot. Oh, come now! That's another matter! (*Looks into mirror.*)

Boniface. (*Suddenly the champion.*) She's perfectly right!

Cot. You keep out of this!

(Angelique *moves to Left Center and looks at* Boniface.)

Marcelle. Just you be careful! I may easily look elsewhere for the happiness you've never been able to give me!

Cot. What! You? I'd like to see you find it!

Marcelle. And why not? (*Rises; crosses to* Angelique.) Less attractive women than I have found consolation outside the home!

Cot. (*Crosses Left above sofa to* Boniface.) Well, go

ahead, my dear! See what you can manage. Search around for your consolation!

MARCELLE. (*Crosses Center.*) Oh! Don't you dare me! Don't you dare dare me!! (*Crosses Down Right below sofa.*) If once I make up my mind— I know—lots of men—

COT. Oh!

MARCELLE. —gentlemen—

COT. (*Crosses over to* MARCELLE.) What! Then what's stopping you? Go ahead! Find your gentleman!

ANGELIQUE. (*Crosses to* COT.) Stop it, Cot! You'll drive her too far!

(BONIFACE *breaks over Right.*)

COT. She drives me too far! Let her go to her—her paramour—I hope she finds him, and when she does, he's welcome to keep her!

MARCELLE. Oh! Monsieur Boniface!!! Did you hear that?

BONIFACE. It's madness! You're mad! He's mad!

(ANGELIQUE *hits* BONIFACE *on chest.*)

MARCELLE. (*Crosses and sits sofa.*) Very well then, you've asked for it!

COT. (*Crosses below sofa to door Up Left.*) I certainly have! Good-evening.

ANGELIQUE. (*Crosses—follows him.*) Now, come along, Cot! Give her a kiss and make it up.

COT. Kiss her? Certainly not! (*He moves upstage.*)

(BONIFACE *follows to the door.*)

ANGELIQUE. (*Lifting skirts.*) Oh, Cot! Monsieur Cot!!! (*She follows him out Up Left.*)

BONIFACE. (*Following to the door.*) You're making a

big mistake, Henri—a big mistake! (*Closes Up Left door.*)

MARCELLE. (*Sitting on sofa.*) Just listen to the way he talks to me—my own husband—just listen to him.

BONIFACE. Marcelle, I love you! (*Crosses to above sofa.*)

MARCELLE. (*Rising.*) Eh?

BONIFACE. You heard me warn him. I tried to stop him. You can't say I didn't do my duty as a friend, can you?

MARCELLE. No.

BONIFACE. I told him, you're making a big mistake, Henri, he wouldn't listen. Well, that's his funeral. All I know is when you threatened to find consolation elsewhere, he said "Find it." Well, Mme. Cot, as a woman of character you must find your consolation at once.

MARCELLE. Yes. Yes. You're right. (*Sitting sofa.*)

BONIFACE. (*Crosses Right above sofa to Right of MARCELLE.*) And you cannot say there is no one to hand. I am here.

MARCELLE. You?

BONIFACE. Certainly. I (*Crosses above sofa to Left Center.*) never permit a lady to be insulted in my presence. He dared you. I accept the dare. I will be your lover.

MARCELLE. You?

BONIFACE. (*Kneels Left end of sofa.*) Marcelle, I am the last man in the world to betray a friend. It hurts me deeply.

MARCELLE. I know that, Boniface.

BONIFACE. But, friend or no friend, the honor of French chivalry is at stake. Marcelle, be mine—all mine!

MARCELLE. (*She leans back and fights off BONIFACE.*) Oh, M. Boniface, you forget yourself. I'm a respectable married woman. Think of my duty.

BONIFACE. There are times when duty must be forgotten.

MARCELLE. When?

BONIFACE. (*Straightens up.*) Now! Look at me. Am I not throwing my duty to the wind? Think of poor Mme. Boniface, but do I hesitate? No, because a greater duty lies before us.

MARCELLE. Yes! Yes!

BONIFACE. We have been insulted and when a man is insulted there is no turning back.

MARCELLE. No! No!

BONIFACE. (*Takes her left wrist.*) Forward march!

MARCELLE. Where?

BONIFACE. (*Pulling her toward Left.*) Anywhere! Together! Let us go!

(BOTH *rising and crossing to door, Left.*)

MARCELLE. (*Breaks away Right above sofa.*) No, M. Boniface, I cannot!

BONIFACE. You hesitate? (*Follows her.*) Oh Marcelle, have you forgotten the public outrage you have just endured?

MARCELLE. (*Right of* BONIFACE.) I shall never forget it.

BONIFACE. You talk of your duties. Does he give a thought to his duties as a husband— as a man?

MARCELLE. That's true.

BONIFACE. His neglect has set you free!

MARCELLE. Absolutely!

BONIFACE. (*Dabs her eyes with her handkerchief.*) He has the prettiest little wife in the world and he leaves her here vegetating like a cabbage.

MARCELLE. Yes, it's true. A cabbage, that's me— (*Snatches handkerchief.*) that's mine.

BONIFACE. Revenge is yours! It must be swift and deadly.

MARCELLE. That's it! Revenge! (*Sitting Right end of sofa.*) Thank you for showing me what I must do.

BONIFACE. I'll show you what a man should be—

strong, tender, and terrible in his passion! (*Pushing* MARCELLE *back on sofa; he kneels above sofa.*)

MARCELLE. Well, M. Boniface, you may be rather plain, but you do have a way with women!

BONIFACE. (*Rises.*) Oh, Marcelle, thank you! Thank you for that!

MARCELLE. Heaven knows that an hour ago I would have repelled your advances with horror!

BONIFACE. (*Crosses to Down Left.*) Oh, Marcelle! The early bird doesn't always catch the worm!

MARCELLE. (*Rises, to Center.*) But now I say: "Command me— I shall obey!"

BONIFACE. (*Crosses Up Center, toward her; embracing her.*) Oh, Marcelle, I'm floating!—floating!— (*Takes her in his arms.*)

ANGELIQUE. (*Offstage.*) Boniface!

BONIFACE. (*To front.*) We're sunk! (*Following MARCELLE, who has moved away.*) There isn't a second to be lost—your husband is away tonight—you're free as air— I shall manage to be free as air too—

MARCELLE. Do!— Do!

BONIFACE. (*Up Center; airily.*) I shall meet you somewhere—

MARCELLE. (*Practical.*) Where?

BONIFACE. I haven't the faintest idea— I'll find somewhere— (*One step to her*) and let you know— And then—revenge! Psst!— My wife!!

(*He leaves* MARCELLE *and scuttles back to his worktable.* MARCELLE *runs Down Right to desk.*)

ANGELIQUE. (*Entering.*) Well, really, our friend Cot has most extraordinary manners, I must say! (*Crosses to sofa and sits Left end.*)

BONIFACE. In what way?

ANGELIQUE. I was only trying to patch things up, out of the kindness of my heart, and do you know what he

said? "Keep your big face out of this, and mind your
own business."

MARCELLE. Typical!

BONIFACE. (*Unconvinced*.) Not very nice!

ANGELIQUE. Nice!— I should think not, indeed!

BONIFACE. And to you.

ANGELIQUE. Exactly!

BONIFACE. An older woman!

ANGELIQUE. That is *not* the point! (*To* MARCELLE.)
Oh, my dear—my heart bleeds for you—with such a
husband!

MARCELLE. (*Forgetting*.) Well!— We'll soon see about
that!

ANGELIQUE. About what?

MARCELLE. Oh, nothing—nothing—

ANGELIQUE. If ever Boniface took it into his head to
behave like that to me—

BONIFACE. (*Coming down Center*.) What then, my
dear?

ANGELIQUE. I wouldn't waste a second!

MARCELLE. What would you do?

ANGELIQUE. Do? Throw myself into the arms of the
first man that came my way!

BONIFACE. (*Steps down*.) Oh, Angelique!!— You
wouldn't!!

ANGELIQUE. I most certainly *would!!*

BONIFACE. (*Step down; to front*.) He'd be crushed to
death! (*Return to trestle table*.)

VICTOIRE. (VICTOIRE *enters Up Left with the morning
mail on a tray*.) The post, Madame, (*Crosses to* AN-
GELIQUE.) and someone is here with a new hat for Mme.
Cot. (VICTOIRE *exits Up Left*.)

MARCELLE. Oh yes— I ordered it only yesterday—
Will you excuse me?

ANGELIQUE. Of course!— There's nothing like a new
hat to help you when your marriage is on the rocks! Au
revoir, my dear!

MARCELLE. Au revoir! (*Up to Right of* BONIFACE; *to*

BONIFACE.) Au revoir, you! (*Crosses Left below* BONI-
FACE.)

BONIFACE. (*Aside.*) It's a bargain?

MARCELLE. (*Close to Left of* BONIFACE. *Aside.*) Yes!
(*Crosses to door Up Left. As she goes.*) Cot's asked for
it, *and* he's going to get it!

(MARCELLE *exits.* ANGELIQUE *sits desk Down Right and
examines mail.*)

BONIFACE. (*To himself.*) Now to find a discreet little
rendezvous! But where?— (*He knocks on the table with
suppressed excitement—giggles.*) Of course!— The telephone directory!!

ANGELIQUE. Come in!
    (*She looks at the door.* BONIFACE *on to high stool.*)
Oh dear! I shall be dining out this evening—

BONIFACE. (*Aside.*) Perfect! (*To his wife.*) Where are
you off to, love?

ANGELIQUE. To my sister's in Versailles. She isn't well!
If she's no better when I get there I may stay the night.

BONIFACE. (*Aside.*) Better still!!

ANGELIQUE. I'm afraid you will be on your own for
dinner!

BONIFACE. (*Looking through the telephone book, his
back to his wife.*) Ha— He— Hi— Ho— Hotels!—

ANGELIQUE. (*Opening another letter.*) Oh dear! The
dressmaker's bill!

BONIFACE. (*Loudly.*) Got it!!

ANGELIQUE. Got what?

BONIFACE. What?— Oh—you've got your bill.

ANGELIQUE. That's what I said!

BONIFACE. So did I!

ANGELIQUE. Why?

BONIFACE. Oh—well—just to show an interest, my
dear!

ANGELIQUE. Ridiculous!

BONIFACE. (*Aside.*) What a beast! (*Aside, reading*

directory.) Hotel— Temperance Hotel—no— Bull and Cow— Dear me, no—

ANGELIQUE. Good gracious me— How disgraceful!

BONIFACE. What is?

ANGELIQUE. It's an outrage!— Sending out these things!

BONIFACE. What things?

ANGELIQUE. Circulars for hotels!— One, two, three of them!!

BONIFACE. (*Puts telephone book on Up Left desk.*) Circulars?

ANGELIQUE. It ought to be prohibited! Listen to this. "Sleep in security. Hotel Paradiso. Recommended to people who are married. Together or separately."

BONIFACE. Together or separately. Does it really say that?

ANGELIQUE. See for yourself! (*Hands him one of the circulars.*)

BONIFACE. So it does!

ANGELIQUE. A philanderer's paradise, I'll be bound!

BONIFACE. Tt—tt—tt— (*Aside.*) The very thing! (*Reading aloud.*) "Rooms at all prices!"

ANGELIQUE. (*Continuing to read from one of the remaining circulars.*) "Large discount for seasonal bookings!" Abominable!

BONIFACE. Abominable is the word! (*Aside.*) I'll book a seasonal! (*He pops circular in his pocket.*)

ANGELIQUE. What do they take me for, sending me an advertisement like that!! (*She crumples the remaining circulars and throws them on the floor.*)

VICTOIRE. (*Entering Up Left.*) Madame, there's a gentleman here asking to see you and M. Boniface.

ANGELIQUE. What sort of gentleman?

VICTOIRE. Here's his card. (*Gives her card.*)

ANGELIQUE. Ah, M. Martin— Boniface, it's our old friend Martin.

BONIFACE. Really! Martin?— Up from Valence, then?—

ANGELIQUE. (*Rising.*) All right, Victoire—ask him to come right up.

VICTOIRE. Very well, Madame.

ANGELIQUE. Oh—and Victoire, pick those papers off the floor, please.

VICTOIRE. (*Picking up the crumpled circulars.*) Yes, Madame. Circulars! Will you be wanting them?

ANGELIQUE. Wanting them? Certainly not! Take them away!

VICTOIRE. Very well, Madame. (VICTOIRE *exits Up Left, looking at them.*)

ANGELIQUE. Martin in Paris—the dear fellow!

BONIFACE. It'll be nice to see him after all that charming hospitality he showed to us in Valence.

ANGELIQUE. He couldn't have been more hospitable, putting us up for two whole weeks—such good food, too!!

BONIFACE. And behaved as though we were doing *him* the favor!

ANGELIQUE. As though he were the guest, and we the hosts—and what a brilliant talker!

BONIFACE. Naturally, my dear, he's a lawyer.

(VICTOIRE *shows* M. MARTIN *into the room.*)

VICTOIRE. Come in, Monsieur.

(MARTIN *enters. Pop-eyed, with a large mustache and no chin; long legs and, at the moment, a strained manner.*)

BONIFACE. Well, well, well!— Come in, come in—my dear Martin!

ANGELIQUE. What a lovely surprise!

(MARTIN *embraces her.*)

BONIFACE. How nice of you to come! May I have your

hat and umbrella. My dear old chap, you're soaked to the skin! (*Takes* MARTIN'S *umbrella and places it near the window.*)

ANGELIQUE. Do sit down and make yourself at home.

MARTIN. Oh, my dear friends, I was lo-lo— I was lo-lo—

BONIFACE. What's that?

MARTIN. I say I was lo-lo-looking forward to seeing you again!

ANGELIQUE. You must be tired, my dear M. Martin. Won't you sit down?

MARTIN. (*Sitting, Left end of sofa.*) But— I am— hohohohoho—

BONIFACE. (*Down to Right of* ANGELIQUE.) What on earth's the matter with him?

MARTIN. You must admit you didid—you dididn't dididn't - expect toto see me.

BONIFACE. (*Crosses above to Right end of sofa; to* MARTIN.) For heaven's sake, M. Martin, what's the matter? Has something happened to you?

MARTIN. Wawawa—why?

BONIFACE. Well—er—it seems to me—that—it's not very noticeable of course—but you have—well, a slight difficulty in speaking!

ANGELIQUE. But when we were staying with you we never noticed anything peculiar—on the contrary.

MARTIN. Ah—last sumsumsumsum—summer—didduddud—during those two weeks—the wewewewe—weather was susu—was susu—

BONIFACE. Whe weather was so-so?

MARTIN. Wait, I haven't fifififififi—finished! The weather was su—su— (*He kicks out and shouts.*) PERB!

BONIFACE *and* ANGELIQUE. (*At a loss and startled.*) Yes—yes, of course!

MARTIN. When the wewewe—weather is sususu—

BONIFACE. Perb!

MARTIN. I speak—er—er—like anyone else!

ANGELIQUE. Ah, come now!

MARTIN. When, like today—it rains—caca—caca—

BONIFACE. Cabbages?

MARTIN. No—cats and dogs!!——

BONIFACE. It'll come—it'll come—

MARTIN. Immediately my little imp—my little imp—

BONIFACE. Your little imp?—

MARTIN. My little imp—ediment comes on!

ANGELIQUE. How very peculiar!

BONIFACE. A walking barometer!

MARTIN. But when there's a hurri—hurri—hurricane—not a word comes out!

BONIFACE. What? Dumb?

MARTIN. It's dam—dam—dam—

BONIFACE. (*With a look at* ANGELIQUE.) Yes, yes—of course!

MARTIN. Dam—damaging to my whole career.

ANGELIQUE. I should think so! My poor friend— As a lawyer—how do you manage to plead?

MARTIN. When—it rains?—we-well— I ask for an ad—for an ad—

BONIFACE. —vertisement?

MARTIN. —journment! (*He kicks out in irritation.*)

BONIFACE. (*Jumping back in fright.*) Then you can't make much of a living in the rainy season?

MARTIN. A totototo—total loss.

BONIFACE. (*Shaking* MARTIN's *hand.*) Well, anyway, my dear Martin, it's extremely nice to see you. I must be the first friend you have called on!

MARTIN. Aha—dear Boniface— I knew with you—a cocold—a co—cold—

BONIFACE. Who, me?

MARTIN. A cocold—reception would be out of the question!

BONIFACE. Aha! Good!—Good!

ANGELIQUE. Dear M. Martin—always a gracious word!

MARTIN. (*With a waggish look.*) Ah, Mme. Boniface, you're not sli—sli— (*He kicks.*)

ANGELIQUE. Not sly?

MARTIN. Sli—sliding out of your invitation as easily as thathatha—that— I haven't forgotten what you said to me last summer— "If ever you come to Paris—you must stastastay with us."

BONIFACE. (*Crosses to Right of* MARTIN.) Yes! Yes, of course!

ANGELIQUE. But this is a delightful surprise!

BONIFACE. Stay as long as you like—two, three days— Do stay at least three days!

MARTIN. Oh, no!

BOTH BONIFACES. Oh, yes! Please do!

MARTIN. Oh, nnnno!

BONIFACE. Martin— I shall be cross!

ANGELIQUE. Yes, we shall!

MARTIN. No!— A momomomonth!

BOTH BONIFACES. A month!

BONIFACE. Aha!— Yes—that *will* be nice!

ANGELIQUE. (*Rather less warmly.*) Very nice indeed!

MARTIN. So here I am— I simply arrived—without any fuss—to stay with you!

ANGELIQUE. It's charming of you, so unexpected.

MARTIN. I've been looking forward to the privi—to the privi—

ANGELIQUE. To the what?

MARTIN. To the privilege.

ANGELIQUE. Too kind of you.

MARTIN. Not at all.

BONIFACE. (*Dubiously.*) Well, we're very happy—very happy indeed!

(MARTIN *bows and goes upstage to take off his overcoat.*)

ANGELIQUE. (*Aside to her husband.*) A month!— Rather a long time— (*Walks to Left of* BONIFACE.) We only stayed two weeks!

BONIFACE. There were two of us! It all mounts up!
    (*As* MARTIN *comes downstage.*)
Good old Martin!

MARTIN. I hope I'm not putputputting you out?

BONIFACE. (*Down Right of sofa.*) No, not at all! And in any case you won't take up much room—a simple bachelor like you—with just a suitcase!

MARTIN. Ah!—but I've brought a surprise for you!

ANGELIQUE. A surprise! How delightful!— He thinks of everything!

VICTOIRE. (VICTOIRE *enters Up Left.*) Madame, they are bringing in a trunk!

MARTIN. That'll be mine!

BONIFACE. Ah! Your baggage!

(A PORTER *enters with a trunk on his back.*)

PORTER. Here's the goods!

(VICTOIRE *exits Up Left.*)

MARTIN. Will you kindly leleleave—leave—it here? (*He kicks out.*)

PORTER. Right you are!

(BONIFACE *helps him to lower it to the floor.*)

MARTIN. How much is that?

PORTER. Fifty francs.

(MARTIN *pays him. He exits.*)

ANGELIQUE. (*Gazing at the trunk.*) But, good heavens, what an enormous trunk!

BONIFACE. (*Peering around it.*) It's monumental! Well, well, it had better be taken to your room.

VICTOIRE. (VICTOIRE *enters Up Left, speaking to someone outside the door.*) This way, please! Madame, there are some more porters here with some more luggage!

BOTH BONIFACES. More!!

(*Four* PORTERS *enter with four trunks on their backs.*)

MARTIN. Ah! Those are mine, too!

ANGELIQUE. Yours? One, two, three, four—but I don't understand—

MARTIN. This is where the surprise begins!

ANGELIQUE. Whatever can you be bringing us in all that? (*To* BONIFACE.) What can it be?

BONIFACE. It must be something very special to fill five trunks!

MARTIN. (*To* BONIFACE.) Look, I have no change—be a good chap and give something to these por—popo—por—por—

BONIFACE. (*Glumly; rhythmically.*) —ter—ters!! (*Gets the money out.*) There we are!— Now, my good man—go on down to the kitchen and you'll each get a glass of wine.

PORTERS. Thank you, Monsieur— (*Etc. They go out Up Left.*)

BONIFACE. (*As they go, looking at the trunks.*) Five trunks full of surprise! They certainly do things on a large scale in the provinces—a very large scale!

ANGELIQUE. Let's open them now!

MARTIN. W-wh-why?

BONIFACE. Why?— Well, to get the surprise!

MARTIN. Oh, no!— No, no, no!

BONIFACE. He wants to keep us in suspense.

MARTIN. Pay—pay—pay— (*He gives a huge kick.*) Patience!

BONIFACE. (*Jumping, to avoid the kick.*) Oh! What *can* it be?

ANGELIQUE. M. Martin, you want us to be in suspense. Well, we *are* in suspense! And, of course, very, very grateful! So now!— (*She looks expectantly at the trunks.*)

BONIFACE. (*After a pause.*) I've known people to be generous in my day—but generosity on this scale reaches a point of real insocem—incomsemm—incommen—

MARTIN. (*Calmly.*) Incommensurability.

(BONIFACE *shakes his hand.*)

BOTH BONIFACES. Bravo!

MARTIN. I never stutter for other people!!

VICTOIRE. (*Entering Up Left.*) Madame, there are some young ladies who have just come straight from the omnibus and are asking—

MARTIN. (*Going to the door.*) Ah—that'll be for me— let them come in!

VICTOIRE. Very good, Monsieur!

BONIFACE. Young ladies? Who are they?

MARTIN. (*Turning triumphantly to the* BONIFACES.) Ah! ha! ha! That's *it!* That's the surprise!

BOTH BONIFACES. What is?

MARTIN. You don't know my d-d-d-daughters, do you?

BONIFACE. No!

MARTIN. I was a lonely bachelor when you were with me last summer—because ever since the death of poor Mme. Martin—oh, eight years ago—my d-d-daughters have been brought up in a convent— But they've just closed it down— So I said to myself—the Bonifaces have never met the children— I'll give them a surprise— I'll bring my daughters with me!

BOTH BONIFACES. What??

MARTIN. I arrived first to tell you they were coming!

ANGELIQUE. Do you mean—*they* are the surprise?—

MARTIN. (*Delighted.*) Why, of course!

BONIFACE. Yes, but—but what about the trunks?

MARTIN. My daughters' luggage!

BOTH BONIFACES. (*Astounded.*) It's not possible!

(VOICES *are heard offstage.*)

MARTIN. Here they are! Come along in! Come along in!

(Four Daughters *appear, walking in twos. Pig-tails, straw hats, gloves, etc.*)

Come on in, my chil—chil—chil—chil—

GIRLS. (*All together.*) —Dren! (*Slightly bending forward.*)

MARTIN. You know how often I've spoken to you of my friends, M. and Mme. Bonny—Bonny—Bonny—

GIRLS. (*Together.*) FACE!! (*Slightly bending forward.*)

MARTIN. Exactly! Well—here they are! Go and give them a kiss.

GIRLS. (*Running to* BONIFACE. *In unison.*) How do you do, M. Boniface!! (*Then to* ANGELIQUE.) Hullo, Mme. Boniface!!

BOTH BONIFACES. (*Holding off the attack.*) Yes, yes! Delightful!—enchanting—but—

ANGELIQUE. It's an invasion—an invasion!

(*The* GIRLS *return to* MARTIN.)

BONIFACE. A stampede!

ANGELIQUE. We never knew you had so many daughters!

MARTIN. (*Pleased with himself.*) All mine!

BONIFACE. What are you going to do with them? Are they en route for another convent?

MARTIN. Oh dear me, no!

BONIFACE. But where will they stay?

MARTIN. Well—here!

ANGELIQUE. Here?

BONIFACE. Here? Oh, no, no, my dear fellow. Out of the question!

(*The* GIRLS *are listening intently.*)

MARTIN. But you yourself said—

BONIFACE. Oh yes, I know—I know, my dear fellow, I

said "Do stay with us"—everyone says that—it's a form of politeness!

MARTIN. Oh!

BONIFACE. You took me at my word. Good! You came. Fine!—But not enmasse, like this—with a battalion! What do you think this house is—a barracks?

MARTIN. If I thought this was a ba—ba—barracks, I wouldn't bring my da—da—daughters here!

BONIFACE. (*Getting heated.*) It's extraordinary behavior. Do you hear! (*Prodding him with his finger.*) Extraordinary! Behaviour! (*To* ANGELIQUE.) He thinks we keep a boarding-house!

ANGELIQUE. (*It is now an open fight.*) It's all your fault! Being so free with your invitations!

BONIFACE. My fault—I like that! You are the one who said: "We've *got* to do it! We've spent fifteen days with him, and we can't get out of inviting him!"

ANGELIQUE. (*Right of sofa to Center. Indicating* MARTIN.) I only said that because I thought he wouldn't accept.

BONIFACE. (*Crosses below sofa to Right end.*) Well, it's not my fault that he *did* accept!

(*The* GIRLS *sit down on the trunks.*)

ANGELIQUE. Of course it's your fault! If you had been content to ask him politely—in an offhand sort of way—*you* would have made the gesture, and *he* would never have come! But, oh no! You had to *insist!* You kept on and on at it—till in the end the poor wretch simply *had* to come!

BONIFACE. Of course!— Of course!— (*To* MARTIN.) I might have known it would be my fault!!

MARTIN. (*Getting to his feet, resignedly.*) Yes— Well—if I understand coco—correctly—we had all better move on!

ANGELIQUE. I'm afraid so. There simply isn't room for all of you!

MARTIN. Good! Well, children—off we go! Thank M. and Mme. Boniface.

(*The* GIRLS *and* MARTIN *surround* M. *and* MME. BONI-
FACE *with cries of "Thank you, M. Boniface!"*
"Thank you, Mme. Boniface!" etc. They shake their
hands.)

BONIFACE. No, no, no! Don't mention it. Nothing at all! (*To* MME. BONIFACE.) Angelique, if the porters are still in the kitchen ask them to take away the trunks.

ANGELIQUE. I'll try to catch them. (*She hurries Up Left.*)

(MARCELLE *enters Up Left.*)

MARCELLE. Good heavens! What are all these trunks doing here?

ANGELIQUE. (*On her way out.*) I'm just going to see about having them taken away. (*She exits.*)

MARTIN. (*Seeing* MARCELLE, *and bowing to her.*) Madame!

(*Pause.*)

BONIFACE. (*Quickly presenting the Martins.*) My dear, this is M. Martin, an old friend of mine— And his— er—descendants. (*To* MARTIN.) This is Mme. Cot.

MARTIN *and* CHILDREN. How do you do, Mme. Cot?

(MARTIN *up to trestle table.*)

BONIFACE. (*Aside to* MARCELLE.) I've found what we were looking for! You won't change your mind?

MARCELLE. Never!

BONIFACE. Wait for me this evening at eight o'clock at the corner of the Avenue du Bois and the Rue de la Pompe. Wait in a carriage with the blinds down.

MARTIN. (*To* BONIFACE.) If only I knew of a good hotel. Where do you think we can find somewhere to stay?

BONIFACE. (*Starts feeling in pockets and takes out circular. Turning his head.*) In a minute. I'll be with you in a minute.

MARCELLE. (*Low voice, to* BONIFACE.) Where are we going?

BONIFACE. (*Over to Right of* MARCELLE *and shows her circular.*) The Hotel Paradiso, 220 Rue de Provence.

MARTIN. (*Hearing this, and thinking he has been answered.*) Ah! Thank you! Well, that settles that, children— (*To* BONIFACE.) Well, then—au revoir, Boniface!

(BONIFACE *puts circular back into pocket.* ANGELIQUE *enters with* PORTERS *who start removing trunks.*)

GIRLS. Au revoir, M. Boniface! Au revoir, Mme. Cot! Au revoir, Mme. Boniface!

ANGELIQUE. Goodbye, children! Excuse me, I'm rushing off to my sister's. (*Exits Up Left.*)

MARCELLE. Au revoir!

MARTIN. Mme. Cot! My compliments! (*He goes to the door; turns to* BONIFACE.) See you soon—and thanks— We shall definitely go there!

BONIFACE. Ah! Good, then—off you go!

(*The* PORTERS, *the* MARTINS *and* ANGELIQUE *have gone.*)

BONIFACE. (*Turning excitedly to* MARCELLE.) Oh, Marcelle, you don't know how happy I am! I'm the hap-hap-hap—

MARCELLE. Do be serious!

BONIFACE. Has your husband left?

MARCELLE. Yes—he hardly said goodbye— (*The light of battle in her eye.*) I'll show him. (*To Down Right.*)

BONIFACE. (*Goes Center.*) So will I!

MARCELLE. (*Returns to above Right end of sofa.*) You will!— You must!

BONIFACE. (*Runs back up to* MARCELLE. *Extravagant.*) Oh, I'm the happiest man in the world— Listen, Marcelle, my wife is dining out— (*Takes* MARCELLE'S *hands.*) your husband has left—what do you say to a little dinner together— (*Backs away.*) in a restaurant?

MARCELLE. Yes. (*Up to* BONIFACE.) A public restaurant!— That would really settle it. Our revenge would be complete!

BONIFACE. Well, run along now and get dressed!

(MARCELLE *crosses below him to Left; he passes at her derriere.*)

In half-an-hour at the Rue de la Pompe!

MARCELLE. I'm off!

(*She turns to go—turns back. He blows her a kiss. She waves, and goes to the Up Left door.* ANGELIQUE *enters, followed by* VICTOIRE, *who carries a tray with food on it.*)

ANGELIQUE. Are you leaving, my dear?

MARCELLE. Yes, I have a slight headache!

ANGELIQUE. Well, look after yourself! (*Up to Left Center. To* VICTOIRE.) Put it over there, Victoire!

(MARCELLE *puts tray on trestle table and goes out Up Left.*)

BONIFACE. (*Sitting on his stool.*) What's that?

ANGELIQUE. Your dinner. Victoire has to take Maxime back to his school.

BONIFACE. My dinner?

(VICTOIRE *exits Up Left.*)

(*Getting up, offhand.*) On second thoughts, I don't think I'll dine here this evening! You are going to your sister's— (*To Right of sofa.*) I shall be on my own— I think I shall treat myself to a nice little dinner at a restaurant!

ANGELIQUE. (*Walks Center.*) You'll do nothing of the sort! I won't allow it!

BONIFACE. Why? What's wrong in that?

ANGELIQUE. Because you're a married man. Married men do not eat in restaurants without their wives!

BONIFACE. Is that so?

ANGELIQUE. I should think not, indeed! What would people think if they saw you in a restaurant?

BONIFACE. What do you think they would think?

ANGELIQUE. The day you choose to go to a restaurant, you are going there with me! Tonight you're dining (*Gesture.*) at home. (*Goes Left.*)

BONIFACE. (*To Center, below sofa. Heatedly.*) When are you going to stop treating me as a child!

ANGELIQUE. (*Turns and goes Center.*) What's that you say?

BONIFACE. I say that I've had enough of it!— And whether you like it or not, tonight I am dining in a restaurant! (*He stamps his foot.*)

ANGELIQUE. Oh, no, you won't!

BONIFACE. Oh yes, I will!

ANGELIQUE. You won't!

BONIFACE. I will!

ANGELIQUE. (*Walking toward door Up Left.*) We'll soon see about that! (*She takes the key from the door.*)

BONIFACE. (*Follows her; trying to get it back.*) Here, give that to me! Give that to me!

(ANGELIQUE *pushes him back, he trips and collapses.*)

ANGELIQUE. I'll do nothing of the kind! Don't you come near me! (*Pushes* BONIFACE *towards sofa; he falls into it.*)

BONIFACE. Give it to me! Give me that key!

ANGELIQUE. I won't.

BONIFACE. (*Going up to her again.*) You will!

ANGELIQUE. (*Taking a hatpin from her hat and lunging at him to keep him at bay.*) Never! On guard! There! (*Fencing position.*) —And there! (*Goes Right and into position again.*)

>(BONIFACE *becomes dignified and turns in shocked surprise to the audience.*)

(*Lunging from behind.*) And there!

BONIFACE. Oh, la, la!

>(ANGELIQUE *exits Up Left and slams the door.*)

Let me out! (*He runs to the door and shakes the handle.*) Let me out!

ANGELIQUE. (*Off-stage.*) Goodnight, M. Boniface! See you in the morning!

(*Sound of* BOLT *being shot.*)

BONIFACE. She's shot the bolt. (*Pauses, then humming with artificial unconcern, he returns to sofa; starts to sniffle weepily.*) She's shot the bolt! Help! Fire! (*His eyes register an inspiration. He raises a finger. He tiptoes to firebox and pulls out a rope ladder. He attaches it to one of the two bars above the window-sill. He raises his leg to climb and then, remembering, comes back into the room and puts on his top hat. He returns to the window and disappears over the ledge.*)

CURTAIN

END OF ACT ONE

ACT TWO

The Hotel Paradiso. The set is divided into three sec-
tions. Right is a bedroom, visible to the audience.
Right of this room and downstage against the wall
is a small round table with a faded table cloth.
Further upstage, in wall Right is a door leading to
a bathroom. In the corner, at angle cutting the
corner, is a fireplace. Backstage, facing the audi-
ence, is a bed covered with an enormous feather
eiderdown, and over this a crochet covering. Above
the bed, Persian curtains hang from the ceiling,
drawn through a mahogany ring. Downstage Left, a
door leads to the hallway. This door opens on-stage
to bedroom. Downstage Center, a wicker chair. The
furniture suggests an old-fashioned fifth-rate hotel.
The wallpaper has an ostrich feather design, and
is none too clean. On the mantelpiece a hideous
globe clock and two candelabras with candles; also
two vases of painted porcelain containing artificial
flowers and feathers. At the head of the bed, a table
and a caraje of water, a glass and sugar bowl. The
stair landing occupies the Center section of the set.
Right, the bedroom door is clearly marked "No. 10."
Upstage Back, the stairs emerge from below, from
Left to Right, and continue on upwards and disap-
pear out of sight. At back on the landing is the door
to a room, facing the public, with "No. 9" clearly
marked on it. On the Left downstage and against
the wall that separates the hallway from the third
room Left, is a keyboard with numbered hooks and
keys. Below this is a small table with drawers and
on which are packets of candles. One candle is in a
holder and lit. In front of the table is a wicker chair.
Upstage of this is a door marked "No. 11," which

leads to bedroom Left. This bedroom forms the third
section of the set. It is bigger than the other, and
looks rather like a dormitory. Against the Right wall
and downstage of the door is a small iron bed, fixed
to the wall. Above the bed hangs a small mirror.
Facing this bed, against the opposite wall, Left, and
downstage, are two more small iron beds. They are
parallel to the footlights and have their heads fixed
to the wall Left. A chair next to the first bed-head.
Upstage of the second bed, a door leading to a bath-
room. Further upstage, angling the corner, there is a
fourth bed along the wall. Backstage Left, facing
the audience, is a door leading to another bathroom,
which opens offstage. Between the bed and bath-
room door, a chair. Alcove in back wall is occupied
by a large wooden bed with white bed curtains, also
drawn through a ring and hanging from the ceiling.
Behind bed-head a chair Right and bedside table.
Center stage of room, a small round table with table
cloth. Blue-grey wallpaper and ceiling. The doors
Left and Right in hallway have locks and keys. The
room Right also has a bolt on the inside of its bath-
room door.

(*It is* 8:30 P.M. *as the* CURTAIN RISES *the rooms*
Right and Left are in darkness. The landing is lit
by two gas jets.)

(ANNIELLO *is sitting in the hallway at the table. He is*
Italian; round as a football and has pointed, waxed
mustaches. He is childish and excitable; when he
is nervous he giggles.)

ANNIELLO. (*Cutting the candles in half and making*
notes in a ledger.) One-a candell plus one-a candell—
(*Breaks candles; throws them in drawer.*) dat make
four-a candell! (*He winks and giggles.*) You tink dat
seem notting, ha?— I'm da manager of dis here hotel

since fifateen years—and sapristy I see plenty! Da comings and da goings!— Oh mamma mia!— (*Breaks.*) Well, in fifateen years, by da doubling of da numbers of da candell I make-a de profit of· di six tousand franc! (*He giggles.*) By di small profit I mak-a di big business!!

(GEORGES *comes from Right on landing, running downstairs. An innocent, oafish young man from the country. A large mouth, cropped hair, and a provincial accent.*)

GEORGES. (*Round-eyed and out of breath.*) Oh Lawd! — Oh good Lawd! Oh, M. Anniello, sur!

ANNIELLO. What's da trouble?

GEORGES. Oh, M. Anniello! Sur! If you'd just seen what Oi just seen!— An' it weren't my fault!— Oi knocked on the door first, like you told me!

ANNIELLO. Well?— Spill-a da bean!

GEORGES. Oi heard a ring from No. 22—so Oi knocked on the door— A voice said "Come in"— Oi came in— and what d'you think Oi saw?

ANNIELLO. What?

GEORGES. (*Looking at* ANNIELLO.) A female—in the noode!

ANNIELLO. So? What of eet?

GEORGES. Do you know what she said?—She said, "Page—bring me a pack of cards"!— What'd you have done, sur?

ANNIELLO. What d'you think? I'd've brought 'er da cards.

GEORGES. What?— With 'er like that—in the noode?!

ANNIELLO. Why not?

GEORGES. Do you call that natural?

ANNIELLO. Natural! A nude woman? Dat's di most natural thing in the hotel business.

GEORGES. Oh, Oi'll never get used to these Paris ways!

ANNIELLO. My boy, you're not in da countryside no

more— You're in da metropolis— And what's more, you're in da Hotel Paradiso!— In a coupla weeks you'll be like me! (*He continues to cut the candles.*) Tak-a di life with di pinch of di salt! Now go and give da knock on Number 9!

GEORGES. Number noine? What do you think she'll have on?

ANNIELLO. No, that's not a lady— It's di Turkish schoolmaster! But dis time we teach *him* da lesson!— Da boss of dis 'ere 'otel say he not-ta pay 'is bill for too damn long. We keep 'is trunk and kick 'im out!— You can go tell him right away! Give 'im da boot!!

GEORGES. 'Oo, me?

ANNIELLO. Dat's what I said!

GEORGES. That Turkish Professor I've heard 'is temper's something terrible! 'E says 'e'll knife the next person who disturbs 'im!

ANNIELLO. Oh, di bark is bigger dan di bite! Go and kick 'im out!

GEORGES. But suppose 'e knifes me?

ANNIELLO. Den you come right back and tell me all abaht it! Get-ta da move on!

GEORGES. Yes, sur! (*Goes up to door No. 9.*) Oh Lawd!— Oi'm not cut out for this sort of work! (*He gives a faint knock.*)

TADU. (*A voice of thunder.*) What do you want!!

GEORGES. (*Jumps back in fright. He peeps round the door which he opens slightly, and creeps round and into the room. As he goes.*) Oi'd rather be back with the lady upstairs!

ANNIELLO. (*Aside.*) Poor boy! When he's 'ad fifateen years in da hotel business like me, he'll be less 'ighly strung!

(*A BELL sounds.*)

(*Gets up; goes to head of stairs Right.*) Dat'll be da passing trade!

(*An imposing LADY, in a plumed hat and veil, enters on*

landing from Right. She is followed by a small
GENTLEMAN *in a top-hat and a scarf which half-*
covers his face. He wears a monocle and an opera
cloak.)

LADY. (*Coming downstairs.*) Is the manager about?

ANNIELLO. (*Ingratiatingly; coming downstairs.*) Ah,
good evening, Signorina! Can I be of help to the Signor
and the Signorina?

LADY. Have you—?

ANNIELLO. (*Coming to Right of* LADY.) Of course we
'ave. (*Honeyed tones.*) I can guess well the requirements
of the Signorina—a nice little nest where the gentleman
will be at 'is ease!—'E is a lucky man to 'ave so beautiful a lady!

LADY. Perhaps you know my work— I am Antoinette!

ANNIELLO. Ah, la belle Antoinette!— Da pride of da
theatre of Mon'martre! Dis is a great privilege for da
Paradiso. All-a da gentlemen talk of la belle Antoinette!

LADY. (*In a low voice.*) He's a Duke! (*Moves slowly
below* ANNIELLO *to Down Right.*)

ANNIELLO. (*Comes Center and leads* MAN *to Left of*
LADY.) Oh! My compliments!— I would recommend to
you da room Number 22!— In room Number 22 da
Crown Princess of Poland stayed when she come 'ere to
spend 'er 'oneymoon with 'er Lord Chamberlain. (*To the*
MAN.) You will feel completely at 'ome there, Signor!

MAN. Oh!

(*There is a sound of raised* VOICES. ANNIELLO *goes up*
and then comes down.)

LADY. What is that?

ANNIELLO. Notting to worry! Just a resident to 'oom
we give da boot!—

(GEORGES *comes rushing out of No. 9 and runs to* AN-
NIELLO.)

GEORGES. Oi told you 'e'd try and knife me!— Oi told you!— 'E won't go till we've given 'im back 'is trunk!

ANNIELLO. What? (*Calling; at bottom of stairs.*) Tabu! Tabu!— Come 'ere a minute!

TABU. (TABU *stands in the doorway to No. 9. He wears a white turban.*) Well!— What is it?

ANNIELLO. My fren'— You see dat dere staircase?— Kindly do me da pleasure of going down dem at da double and getting da 'ell out of 'ere!

TABU. I shall go when you have returned me my trunk—not a minute before!

ANNIELLO. You will get da trunk when we get da money for da bill!— Take no notice. (*Over to Left of* MAN.) Take no notice.

TABU. (*Coming down.*) So that's your game! We'll see whether you change your tune when the Police arrive! (*At bottom step.*)

LADY. The police!

TABU. (*Coming down.*) I'll tell them everything that goes on here!

ANNIELLO. Basta basta!

TABU. (*To the* MAN.) It has to be seen to be believed, what goes on!

MAN. Oh, I say!

ANNIELLO. 'Ave you quite finished?

TABU. (*Pushing* ANNIELLO *away. Down to Left of the* MAN. *He bows to the* MAN.) What a hotel!— It's an old dump— And it's ridden with bugs!

LADY. Bugs!

MAN. Oh, I say!

ANNIELLO. Dat is a lie— We put down da flea powder every day!

TABU. That flea powder? It asphyxiates the clients and fortifies the bugs! And what is more, there are rooms not even habitable!— Haunted by strange spirits!

LADY *and* MAN. Spirits!

ANNIELLO. (*To* TABU, *coming Down to him.*) Will you shut da trap!— Will you shut up!

TABU. (*Pushing* ANNIELLO *upstage.*) Look over there! In that very room (*Pointing to door No. 11.*) demons materialize every night. They shout—scream—hurl things about!— He made it into a dormitory for the servants— And now even they refuse to sleep there!

ANNIELLO. (*Comes to Up Left of* TABU.) It's a lie!

TABU. Is it?

LADY. (*Up toward stairs.*) Scandalous!

MAN. Simply frightful! (*Follows her; going to bottom of stairs.*)

TABU. Can you deny that you have had to call in an expert from the Ministry of Sanitation?— Dare you deny that? (*Twirls* ANNIELLO *away Right.*)

LADY. What an appalling place to find oneself in!— (*To* ANNIELLO.) Sir—you can dispose of Number 22 elsewhere— (*She starts to move off upstairs.*)

ANNIELLO. (*Following her.*) No, no! Signorina—you do not leave?

LADY. I should think we do!— Come, my dear Duke! (*She goes off Right on landing.*)

MAN. (*At top of stairs; turns.*) Oh, I say! (*He follows her.*)

ANNIELLO. (*Runs after them.*) But listen 'ere, Signor— Signorina!— (*To* TABU.) Dat is your 'andywork!

TABU. Exactly! They've gone and I'm going too! (*To his door, No. 9. To* ANNIELLO.) And I warn you, you'll be hearing from me! (*To* GEORGES.) And *you'll* be hearing from me too! (*He goes.*)

ANNIELLO. (*To* TABU's *retreating figure.*) 'Appy journey, my dear chap!— Go and get yourself da boot some place else!

GEORGES. 'E's done us out of two customers!

ANNIELLO. (*At desk.*) To 'ell with da customers. Dey give me da pip!— Anyhow she's an amateur— She can't act for peanuts— (*Sits desk.*) And 'er voice is like when when you tear da sheets! (*Getting up.*) But I'd lik-a to 'ave seen 'ow he made out with 'er! Dat dumb Duke!

GEORGES. (*He comes downstairs.*) 'Ow would you have seen any'ow?

ANNIELLO. What do you mean?

GEORGES. They mightn't have asked you in!

ANNIELLO. (*Pinching his cheek.*) Da big baby, eh? Maybe they do not ask me in—but I 'ear and see everything jus' da same!

GEORGES. 'Ow?

ANNIELLO. 'Ow? (*Shrugs his shoulders.*) Da bambino! (*Opening a drawer and gets up, taking out a drill.*) What you think dat's for?

GEORGES. A drill?— To make 'oles!

ANNIELLO. Perfetto! When something interests me— (*He turns his drill round.*) Tutto! I see it all!

    (*A* BELL *sounds.*)

(*Putting drill on desk.*) Dat's da bell for da business!

    (GEORGES *runs upstairs.*)

COT'S VOICE. (*Off.*) Hello there! —Is there anybody about? Where is the manager? (*He comes into view up the stairs Left.*)

ANNIELLO. (*Going to him. Ingratiatingly.*) Right 'ere, Signor! You are expecting someone, eh? (*Taking* COT *Down Center.*) I can guess exactly da gentleman's requirements—a cosy little nest where the pretty lady will feel at 'er ease! Eh?

COT. (*Holding his suitcase.*) Thank you, no! I am not expecting anyone. You are expecting me. I am M. Cot, the expert appointed by the Board of Sanitation.

ANNIELLO. Ah—si, si, si— Of course— For da haunted room. Ah, Monsieur Cot, it is da pure witchcraft!

    (BELL *sounds.*)

Georges—somebody wants something— Go upstairs and answer da bell.

    (GEORGES *exits Right on landing.*)

Si, si Signor!— Every night dere are di most ghastly sounds— Da walls crack— Da furniture hops in di air!

COT. Just so! Just so! There is no need to elaborate, since I am here to examine the evidence and see for myself. Where is this room?

ANNIELLO. (*Pointing Left.*) Right dere, Signor!— If you will allow me to light-a da candell. (*He does so. Opens door No. 11.*)

COT. Well, let us look at this haunted chamber!

(*They enter the room No. 11.*)

ANNIELLO. I am glad dat it ees you dat ees sleeping da night 'ere and not-ta myself! (*Shuts door, puts candle on table.*)

COT. (*Smiling, walks around the table past Center of room.*) It seems strangely quiet for a room in which spirits are supposed to cavort!

ANNIELLO. Aha!— Eet is quiet enough at dis time of da night!— But when da midnight strike—den starts da hull-ba-loo!

COT. I see! Phantoms of disorderly and rowdy nature, eh? (*He laughs. Crosses to alcove.*)

ANNIELLO. Ah, Signor— You are da expert—but da expert will laugh at di other side of da face!

(*There is the sound of* SINGING *upstairs.*)

COT. Noises already? The ghosts seem to be making an early start this evening! (*Crosses down to table.*)

ANNIELLO. Non, non, non, Signor!— Dat's di salesmen from de Bon Marche stores—with dere—sales ladies!—from time to time dey get a little out of hand! Ah, da youth! It is natural— I will go and tell them to keep quiet. (*Going out.*)

COT. Off you go then! (*He puts down his case and opens it.*) —Let's see now—cigars—brushes— (*He takes things from his bag and sets them out on the table.*)

(SONG: "*LA PETITE TONKINOISE.*")

ANNIELLO. (*At the stairs, shouting.*) 'Ave you quite finished up there?

VOICES. (*From above.*) No!!

ANNIELLO. No!?— Is dat so?— Wait! I come up! I shut your trap!

BONIFACE. (*Appears from stairs Left, wearing his top-hat, smoking a cigar, and carrying Marcelle's suitcase. Nervously.*) Excuse me!— Are you the manager?

ANNIELLO. One momento, Signor!— I am with you in a momento! (*He runs upstairs and off Right.*)

BONIFACE. (*Turning to* MARCELLE *who has followed him in.*) In a momento— He'll be here in a momento!— My dear, I really think we've hit on a nice quiet little hotel! (*Coming Down to Center.*)

MARCELLE. (*Looking around.*) But it's beastly, your hotel!— How on earth did you come across it? (*Down to Right of* BONIFACE.)

BONIFACE. Of course, its appearance is a little against it— But it's just what we're looking for! In a smart hotel we might have been recognized—whereas here, it would be extremely bad luck if we met anyone we knew.

MARCELLE. That's true!

COT. (*In room No. 11, sneezing.*) Atchou!!

BONIFACE. (*Good-naturedly.*) God bless you! (*Bows.*)

COT. (*Bowing to the door.*) I thank you!

BONIFACE. Don't mention it! (*To* MARCELLE, *tenderly*). Anyway, what matters the hotel, (*Brings her Down Right.*) since it brings the two of us together? (*Change of tone.*) Heavens—what a smell of drains!—

ANNIELLO. (*Re-enters. Coming down.*) Now, Signor—

BONIFACE. Ah! Here's the manager.

(COT *goes into the bathroom upstage. The* LIGHTS *fade, Left.*)

ANNIELLO. Right 'ere, Signor—at your service! (*Very ingratiatingly.*) I canna guess well the requirements for the gentleman— A charming leetle nest where the lady will be at her ease!— She is exquisite, Signor—exquisite!

BONIFACE. The lady is my wife.

ANNIELLO. No!

BONIFACE. Yes.

ANNIELLO. (*With smiling correction.*) No!

BONIFACE. Yes!

ANNIELLO. No!—di gentleman carry da baggage!

BONIFACE. Tell me, have you anything vacant on this floor?

ANNIELLO. (*Crosses to desk, gets candle. Pointing Right.*) Yes, Signor!— Number 10— It was in dis 'ere room dat the Crown Princess of Poland spent 'er 'oneymoon with 'er Lord Chamberlain!

BONIFACE. Perfect! Perfect! (*To* MARCELLE.) The Princess of Poland!— You see—the very best people come here!

(ANNIELLO *goes Right; opens door No. 10; stands in door.* MARCELLE *in first;* BONIFACE *follows.*)

ANNIELLO. (*Holding a lighted candle. Crosses behind them.*) Dere you are, Signor— You will never find a better room!

(*They all enter the room, Right.*)

You see—very comfortable— (*Opens door Right.*) You 'ave da room for washing leading off—very special and convenient. (*Crosses Left back of them; puts candle on table.*)

BONIFACE. Good!— I'll take this room! (*Puts suitcase Down Left.*)

ANNIELLO. Buono— (*He lights the candles in the room.*)

BONIFACE. (*Forgetting* ANNIELLO.) Marcelle! (*Embraces her.*)

MARCELLE. (*Quickly, aside.*) S-s-sh!—the manager!

BONIFACE. Ah!

(*All three show embarrassment.*)
Good—well—I'll take this room!

ANNIELLO. You will not-ta regret!— Good-a-night,
Signor! Good-a night, Signorina! (*Goes into hall.*)

BONIFACE. Good-night. (*Turning rather too impul-
sively to* MARCELLE, *kneels, picks her up by her legs.*)
Aah—Marcelle!!

(COT *re-enters from bathroom and crosses bedroom to go
out.*)

ANNIELLO. (*Suddenly re-entering No. 10.*) Here is
your key, Signor!— I wish you a pleasant evening.
(*Throws key on bed. He exits again to hallway. To* COT,
who is now on stairs.) You go out, Signor?

COT. (*Giving him the candle.*) Yes. It's too early to
go to bed. I shall go to the cafe next door for a glass of
beer— (*He moves up to staircase Left.*)

(MARCELLE *walks up to bed and leaves stole.*)

ANNIELLO. Very good, Signor!

COT. I'll be back in half-an-hour.

ANNIELLO. (*Puts candle on table.*) You will find your
candell right here!

(COT *goes out downstairs Left, while* ANNIELLO *goes upstairs and off Right.*)

BONIFACE. (*In the doorway.*) Marcelle!

MARCELLE. (*A little uncertain.*) Boniface!

BONIFACE. (*Reproachfully; comes Upstage.*) Ah no!
Not Boniface—not any more!— Call me Benedict!

MARCELLE. All right!— Benedict! (*She moves away a
little.*)

BONIFACE. (*Following her.*) Yes, Benedict!— Oh,
Marcelle! The hour of vengeance has sounded—here in

my arms! (*He tries to embrace her again, cigar in mouth.*)

MARCELLE. Be careful!— You'll burn me with that cigar! (*Turns face away.*)

BONIFACE. Wait! Wait!— (*Shifts cigar to Right side of mouth. He again tries to embrace her, forgetting the cigar.*) Marcelle! I adore you!

MARCELLE. (*Holding him off.*) Do be careful!— I'm swallowing your cigar smoke! (*She backs away.*)

BONIFACE. Oh!— Excuse me! I beg your pardon.

MARCELLE. (*Taking off gloves.*) Can't you throw it away?

BONIFACE. Well—they charged me forty sous for it, so I should really smoke it to the end!

MARCELLE. (*Put out.*) Oh well!—in that case—

BONIFACE. (*Going to the fireplace.*) But what of it? Where love is concerned I simply ignore the questions of expense. (*Coming back to* MARCELLE *after putting cigar out in ash tray on mantel.*)

MARCELLE. And what about my dress, eh? How do you like it?

BONIFACE. (*Bold.*) You would look desirable in any dress—and even more desirable out of it! (*Comes to table Down Right.*)

MARCELLE. Oh! Oh!— M. Boniface!— The dress-maker only brought it this evening and I put it on specially for you!

BONIFACE. Who cares about the dress! Does one even glance at the box which contains the bon-bon? (*Passionately.*) Marcelle— It's only you that I see!— You!— I don't *see* your dress!— For me you have no dress!— I want you!— I want you!—

MARCELLE. (*Starts around chair to Right and Up.* BONIFACE *follows.*) Good gracious—whatever's come over you, Monsieur Boniface!— Benedict!— *Please!*

(*Followed by* BONIFACE *around chair again and* MAR-CELLE *over to table and leans.*)

BONIFACE. (*Taking her in his arms.*) I want you, I tell you! I tell you, I want you!

MARCELLE. (*Moving away.*) Whatever's the matter with you? I've never seen you like this! Come now, Benedict!— Pull yourself together!— The champagne must have gone to your head!—

BONIFACE. (*Sits and draws* MARCELLE *on to upstage knee.*) Oh! I don't care what's gone to my head!— (*Bounce.*) It's you!— (*Bounce.*) It's the dinner! (*Bounce.*) the wine!— (*Bounce.*) the cigar!— Oh!—and to think my wife told me that I mustn't smoke and that I mustn't drink wine!— She said it would make me ill!— Well!— Ha! Ha!— Just look at me!— I want you, I tell you!— I want you! (*He sits still, holding* MARCELLE *in his arms.*)

(*The chair gives way and breaks to pieces.*)
Oh!

MARCELLE. (*Rises and steps back, laughing.*) You haven't hurt yourself, have you?

BONIFACE. (*On floor.*) Hurt myself?— No! I did it on purpose! (*Getting up.*) That rotten chair! If they only provide one—they might at least see that it's in a proper condition! (*He throws chair out to the hall.*) Out with you! Out! Out! Out! Beastly thing!

(MARCELLE *turns away and Down.*)
(*Aside.*) Now, where was I? (*Down to Left of* MARCELLE. *Tries to take her in his arms.*) MARCELLE!

(GEORGES *starts downstairs.*)

MARCELLE. (*Gently holding* BONIFACE *off.*) Oh!— If you could only have seen yourself!

BONIFACE. (*Put out.*) *Please,* Marcelle, do stop!

MARCELLE. (*Still shaking.*) You sat there, looking so—minute!

BONIFACE. I assure you—it was nothing to laugh about!

MARCELLE. (*Putting her handkerchief in her mouth.*) Yes!— Yes, my dear—you're right!

BONIFACE. (*Holding her in his arms.*) Oh, my dear!— My own dear! (*He kisses length of her arm; puts her arm around his neck; embraces.*)

GEORGES. (*On the landing, seeing the broken chair.*) Lawd! What's this 'ere?— Number 10's chair— Oi wonder 'oo dun that? (*He marches, humming, into No. 10. Astonished.*) Oh!!! (*Goes above and between* BONIFACE *and* MARCELLE.) Oh—Good Lord!

MARCELLE *and* BONIFACE. (*Separating; he Left; she Right.*) Oh!!!

GEORGES. (*Center. Confused.*) I was puttin' the chair back!

BONIFACE. (*Furious.*) Oh, no, really! This is too much. I've seen quite enough of the damn chair!—and of you, too!— Take it out of here!— Take it out!

GEORGES. But, sur—it belongs in 'ere!

BONIFACE. It does, does it? (*Opens door.*) Well, take it out, do you hear? Out! Out! Out! (*He pushes him into the hallway and slams the door.*) Oh!!!

(*Turns upstage, fixes tie in mirror.* MARCELLE *takes off hat at table; takes off gloves.*)

GEORGES. Something funny going on in there! Oi'd better find out what's up! (*He catches sight of the drill on desk.*) The drill!— Why not?— It's the very thing!

ANNIELLO. (*Off Right, upstairs.*) Georges! Georges!

GEORGES. Coming!— Coming!— (*He puts down the drill and runs upstairs and off Right with broken chair.*)

BONIFACE. (*Left.*) Good Lord!— I'm feeling rather strange!

MARCELLE. (*Steps to him.*) What's the matter?

BONIFACE. I have a cold sensation on the top of my head! It's just emotion— It'll pass. (*Moving to Right of* MARCELLE, *again he lunges into an embrace.*) Oh, Marcelle!— At last we are alone!— Just the two of us!—

Oh, if only you could see how my heart is pounding with love for you!— It's pounding—*pounding!* (*Change of tone.*) Oh, dear—it really *is* pounding!!

MARCELLE. (*Disturbed.*) You've gone quite pale!— Boniface!— Benedict!— Oh, my dear!

BONIFACE. Oh! I feel very peculiar!—very peculiar indeed!

MARCELLE. (*Frightened.*) Sit down, my dear, sit down!

BONIFACE. (*Looking around.*) Where?— Where?— Now there's no chair!

MARCELLE. (*Pointing to Right.*) Oh, well, sit here!— on the table!

BONIFACE. Oh Marcelle— You must excuse this little—er— (*Crosses below her and sits on table.*) setback— It'll soon pass— Oh dear!— Oh dear, oh dear!

MARCELLE. Wait! I'll go and fetch you a glass of water. (*She goes out Right.*)

BONIFACE. (*In despair.*) —It was that cigar!— I knew it! And that champagne— And I never touch anything but water— All those bubbles—

MARCELLE. (*Enters. Stirring some sugar in a glass.*) My poor dear!

BONIFACE. (*Taking sip of water.*) This would happen when my wife's nowhere near to help!

MARCELLE. (*Taking back the glass; goes up to mantel; puts down glass.*) For heaven's sake, do sit still!

BONIFACE. No! I must walk about!— In fact, I think I'd better go out! (*Crosses to door Left.*)

MARCELLE. Yes! Let's both go out! (*Crosses to table to get gloves.*)

BONIFACE. No! No! Alone! I think I must walk by myself in the fresh air— Oh— I'm suffocating!— I can't breathe!

MARCELLE. Well, take your coat off! (*Taking his coat off.*)

BONIFACE. Yes, yes! Oh, good gracious!

(GEORGES *starts downstairs.*)

MARCELLE. Come, now, Benedict, pull yourself together. (*Puts coat on table.*)

BONIFACE. (*Despairing.*) Oh, Marcelle! Something tells me that I'm going to pass away—in this very room!

MARCELLE. (*Alarmed.*) Oh no! Not that— You mustn't do that! (*Over to mantel; dips handkerchief in water and back to* BONIFACE; *wipes his forehead with the wet handkerchief.*)

GEORGES. (GEORGES *has picked up the drill.*) Why not? After all, the boss said so! (*Feeling the Right wall.*) Let's see now— Where shall I make the hole?— Ah— this 'ere looks as if it might give way easy! (*He begins to drill.*)

BONIFACE. (*Now standing against the wall.*) Oh, thank you, my dear!— You are very kind!

GEORGES. (*Outside.*) Oi'll be for it if they twig anything in there—

MARCELLE. Feeling better?

BONIFACE. Not much!

GEORGES. (*Outside, drilling.*) Ah! That's it! 'Ere she goes! Soft as butter!

BONIFACE. (*With a gradual alarm.*) Wait! Oh!— Oh!— Oh!— What can it be?

MARCELLE. (*Backs away.*) What's the matter now?

BONIFACE. I have a sharp sensation at the base of the spine!

MARCELLE. That's a good sign!— The circulation is starting again.

BONIFACE. (*With a scream.*) Ouch!

MARCELLE. What is it?

BONIFACE. (*Leaving the support of the wall, runs Up Right. She follows to Left of him.*) Oh! la, la, la!

GEORGES. (*Removing the drill from the hole.*) That's done it!

BONIFACE. Oh! la, la, la!—Aah!

MARCELLE. (BOTH *Down and then Up.*) Whatever is it?— What do you feel?

BONIFACE. I don't know— I had a sharp stabbing pain as though someone was boring a hole into me!

MARCELLE. Where?

BONIFACE. (BONIFACE *passes* MARCELLE *in front of him and runs to table Down Right.*) At the base of my spine.

MARCELLE. Merciful heavens! It sounds like a cerebral hemorrhage! We should send for a doctor!

BONIFACE. No, no! I just need air— (*He fans himself with Marcelle's hat. Crosses to door below her.*) —and a cup of tea!

GEORGES. (*Outside, on all fours, looking through the the hole.*) Now let's 'ave a peep!

BONIFACE. (*Opening the door.*) Oh, boy!— Where is that boy?— Boy!

> (*He goes Center in hall and sees* GEORGES; *stops.* MARCELLE *in door.*)

What do you think *you're* doing?

GEORGES. (*Aside.*) Lawd! (*Getting up.*) Oi thought I 'eard you call, so Oi was just listening to make sure!

BONIFACE. (*With a tiny voice.*) Boy!— Is there a balcony?— I must have air! (*Moving Up backwards.*)

GEORGES. Next floor up, sur—at the end of the passage—on the roight.

BONIFACE. Thank goodness!

MARCELLE. (*Standing in the doorway, to* GEORGES.) And please bring a hot water bottle for the gentleman!

BONIFACE. (*On stairs.*) Yes, yes! A water bottle. (*Climbing the stairs.*) You'll wait here for me, won't you?

MARCELLE. Yes!

BONIFACE. (*As he disappears.*) You'll never know— how I feel!— (*Going up.*) I'm a very sick man! (*Exits Right.*)

MARCELLE. (*To herself.*) Poor thing! (*To* GEORGES.) Quickly! Get some tisane, some tea—anything!

GEORGES. But, Madame, everything is shut by now— Oh—'alf a minute!— The man we just kicked out—'e made tea every night— 'Is 'ole ruddy equipment's still there. (*He skips into Tabu's room No. 9.*)

(BELL.)

MARCELLE. (*Stepping back into her room; crosses Right.*) Heavens!— What an experience!

GEORGES. (*Re-entering, comes down with the tea apparatus.*) 'Ere we are, 'ere we are—everything to 'and! (*He enters room No. 10, to table.*)

MARCELLE. (MARCELLE *goes with him to above table.*) Good. Put them down there!

GEORGES. (*Putting the things on the table.*) Right, Madame.

(BELL.)

MARCELLE. You don't think the gentleman will catch cold up there on the balcony, do you?

GEORGES. (*Lighting the spirit lamp. Kneeling.*) Oh, no!— It's a mild night out—with a great big yella moon.

MARTIN. (M. MARTIN *appears on the staircase from Left.*) Come along, children!

GIRLS. Coming, Papa!— Coming!

MARTIN. (*Followed by* VIOLETTE, PAQUERETTE, PERVENCHE *and* MARGUERITE.) I've never come across such a hotel— Here we are, up on the first floor and we haven't encountered a single soul! (*Coming down.*) I cannot imagine what induced Boniface to recommend this hotel— But it's no use bringing all our luggage up— Tomorrow we shall move out! (*Cross Up to stairs.*)

PERVENCHE. (*Follows him.*) Yes, I'd rather go to a smart hotel!

VIOLETTE, MARGUERITE, PAQUERETTE. (*Down Center, hopping up and down.*) Me too!— Me too!— Me too!

MARTIN. Porter! Porter!

MARCELLE. (*Watching the water boil on the spirit*

stove, to GEORGES.) Don't forget the gentleman's hot water bottle. (*Goes into bathroom.*)

GEORGES. Yes, Mum. (*Goes in hallway.*)

VIOLETTE. There's the porter.

THE MARTINS. Ah! The porter!

GEORGES. (*Seeing the* MARTIN *brood.*) What's this? A kindergarten?

MARTIN. (*Crosses Down with them.*) Now look here, boy, we were recommended here by M. Boniface.

GEORGES. M. Boniface?— Oh yes, sur!— (*Aside.*) Never 'eard of 'im!—

MARTIN. Now, I would like some accommodation for my daughters and for myself.

GEORGES. Your daughters. (*Aside.*) He must breed like a rabbit!

MARTIN. And what accommodations can you offer?

GEORGES. (*Looking at the key-board.*) Let me see now— Lawd! Oi'm afraid there aren't enough rooms for— (*Aside.*) Oi've got it! The 'aunted chamber! The boss 'as never been able to let it. (*Aloud.*) Look, sur, if you're not too choosey— Oi think Oi might 'ave something for you— (*Gets candle.*)

MARTIN. All right then— Let's see this—er—something!

GEORGES. (*Lights a candle and indicates No. 11.*) This one 'ere, sur. (*He ushers them in.*) 'Ere we are, sur, a nice large room!

MARTIN. (*Going into room.*) But it's a dormitory!

GEORGES. This is all we 'ave, sur!— You have four young ladies and there are just—five beds!

(GIRLS *go to their beds.*)

MARTIN. But I can't share a room with my daughters!

(GIRLS *giggle.*)

GEORGES. (*Indicates alcove.*) Well, sur, if you pop

into bed first you could shut the curtains while the young ladies get into bed—and there are two bathrooms, you know. (*He shows them around.*)

MARTIN. Well, it's highly inconvenient, but it seems there's nothing else for it! (*He takes the candle from* GEORGES.) And what, may I ask, do you charge for this —dormitory?

GEORGES. Well, sur, seeing the circumstances, and as you were sent by M. Whatchermecallit—it'll be twenty francs a day—with no extras!

MARTIN. Well, I must say that's reasonable enough!

MARCELLE. (*Coming out of her bathroom.*) What *can* have happened to Boniface?—

MARTIN. (*To* GEORGES.) Well then, that's settled, my boy. We will take it!— (*He puts his candle on* COT'S *box of cigars.*)

GEORGES. (*Crosses above* MARTIN.) Good, sur!— Good night, sur!— Good night, ladies!

THE GIRLS. Good night, boy!

(GEORGES *goes out to the hallway.*)

MARCELLE. He must be ill!— I'm beginning to get alarmed! (*She goes towards the door.*)

MARTIN. I must get a candle for the girls! (*He goes towards the door.*)

MARCELLE. (*Stepping into hallway.*) I say, boy!

MARTIN. (*Stepping into hallway.*) I say, boy!

(*Together.*)

MARCELLE. (*Turning away, runs Down Right.*) M. Martin!

MARTIN. (*Center, circumnavigating her.*) Unless I'm mistaken—why, yes!— (*Comes Down.*) Why, it's Mme. Cot!

MARCELLE. (*Turning her back.*) No, no, no, no!— Well—as a matter of fact—yes!

(GEORGES *comes Down and to Left.*)

MARTIN. Don't you remember? I had the pleasure of meeting you at the house of our mutual friend, Mr. Boniface!

(*In the room, No. 11, the* GIRLS *are taking off their hats, etc.*)

MARCELLE. (*Very distrait.*) No, no! I assure you, the pleasure was mine!

GEORGES. (*On their Left; crosses above them and into room No. 10. Surprised.*) They're old pals!

MARTIN. What a delightful surprise! (*Calling the* GIRLS.) Children!

MARCELLE. No, no!— I beg you—don't disturb—

MARTIN. But of course— Come here, children!— Look who's here!— It's Mme. Cot!

MARCELLE. (*Runs Down and to front.*) Oh, Lord!— Now he's said my name!

GEORGES. (*At the door.*) So that's 'er name—Mme. Cot! (*Down to above table.*)

GIRLS. (*Entering.*) Mme. Cot!

(GEORGES *goes to attend to the tea.*)

MARCELLE. This is the last straw!

THE GIRLS. (*Rush to her, with cries of joy.*) Oh, Mme. Cot! How lovely! What a surprise! Mme. Cot! Fancy seeing you!

(*They surround her and she acknowledges their greetings with embarrassment.*)

GEORGES. (*From inside the room; above table.*) Mme. Cot—the tea's ready!

MARCELLE. (*Aside.*) —Now *he* knows my name! (*Dis-*

trait.) The tea?— Oh, yes!— Thank you! I heard!
(*Backs up to door.*)

MARTIN. Your *tea?*— But I don't understand— Do
you live here, Madame?

MARCELLE. (*Confused.*) Who, me?— Oh, certainly
not!— That is to say—well—my husband's staying
here— We are moving, you know—from the villa—and
so—for the time being—

GEORGES. Mme. Cot—the water's boiling over!

MARCELLE. (*Aside.*) Oh, I could murder him with his
"Mme. Cot"!

GEORGES. Mme. Cot—the water's— (*Runs past her
and Up.*)

MARCELLE. (*Impatiently.*) Yes, yes!— I heard! Thank
you!— M. Martin, forgive me, but as you see, my kettle
calls!— (*She stands in the doorway.*) I would have liked
to offer you a cup but— (*Goes into Room No. 10; to
Center.*)

MARTIN. (*Following her.*) But that would be delightful— A thousand thanks!

MARCELLE. (*Exasperated.*) Oh!

THE GIRLS. (*Hopping and dancing.*) Yes— Oh yes,
tea! Hurrah for tea!— Tea! Tea! Tea!

MARTIN. (*Coming back to* GEORGES.) Boy— Boy, we
shall want some more cups.

GEORGES. Very good, sur! (*Exits Right, upstairs.*)

MARCELLE. Now I'll never get rid of them!

MARTIN. (*Taking* GIRLS *into room. To* GIRLS.) Come
along now, children— Let's go in and have a nice cup of
tea with Mme. Cot!

MARCELLE. Heavens! His coat! (*She hides Boniface's
coat behind her back.*)

MARTIN. (*Looking around.*) But it's charming in here!

MARCELLE. (*Making for the bathroom.*) Yes! Yes it
is, isn't it?

MARTIN. (*To the* GIRLS *at door.*) Come along in, children!

(MARCELLE *rushes back into room. They troop in.* MAR-
CELLE *has quickly hidden Boniface's hat and jacket
in the bathroom.*)

MARCELLE. (*Forcing herself to be gracious.*) Do sit
down everybody! Do sit down!
MARTIN. We would love to but—er—there seems to
be a slight scarcity of chairs!

(GEORGES *starts downstairs with tray.*)

MARCELLE. (*With a forced laugh.*) You're right.—Oh,
you're right!

(MARTIN *gives forced laugh.*)

GEORGES. (*Runs in.*) 'Ere are the cups! (*He puts down
on table Down Right a tray on which are seven cups and
a sugar bowl.*)
ALL. Ah, good!—at last!
MARTIN. Boy!— We shall need more chairs!
GEORGES. Yes, sur! (*He goes to get them from room
No. 9.*)
MARTIN. Go along, children!— Go and give the boy
hand!

(*They all move out and upstage to the staircase.*)

MARCELLE. (*Aside.*) Heavens, they must go soon!--
Boniface will be back any minute!
MARTIN. (*Steps forward.*) Now, Madame, if you will
allow me, let me fill the pot!
MARCELLE. Oh, yes!— Yes! Thank you, thank you!
GEORGES. (*Re-entering with chairs.*) 'Ere's the chairs!
(*The* GIRLS *come back, each carrying a chair.
Everyone sits down.*)
(*To* MARCELLE.) Oi'll go now and fetch the bottle!
MARCELLE. What bottle?

GEORGES. The 'ot water bottle for the sick gentleman!

MARCELLE. (*With alacrity.*) Oh! Yes, yes!— Off you go!

(GEORGES *goes out Left on landing.*)

(*Aside.*) Oh, this night'll be the death of me! (*Distrait.*) Do sit down, everybody!— Do sit down! (*Takes up pot.*)

MARTIN. (*Settling comfortably in his chair.*) —And tell me, Madame, are things going well with you in general?

MARCELLE. (*Left of table; worried.*) But of course! Everything's going beautifully! (*Pours.*)

MARTIN. (*To his daughters.*) Come along now, children. Make yourselves useful— Serve the tea!

(THEY *busy themselves.*)

(*To* MARCELLE.) And what about our old friend, Boniface?— Do you see a great deal of him?

MARCELLE. Oh, no— Hardly at all!— You know how it is with one's acquaintances in Paris! But his wife is a great friend of mine— That's how I came to be at his house this afternoon.

BONIFACE. (BONIFACE *is seen coming from Right and down the stairs in shirt sleeves. He is gay.*) Oh! I'm feeling much better! A little fresh air and indigestion disappears! I'm a new man!

MARTIN. (*To* MARCELLE.) So you really see very little of him?

MARCELLE. Oh, very little! Very little!

BONIFACE. (*Sings.*)

At the Monaco one dances; one dances.

At the Monaco one dances all the time!

(*Repeats four times.*)

(BONIFACE *enters Room No. 10, at end of song.*)

THE MARTINS. (*Astonished, rising.*) M. Boniface!!

BONIFACE. (*Dumbfounded; swings back into hall.*) The Martins!!

MARCELLE. (*Aside.*) We're done for!

BONIFACE. (*Aside.*) What are *they* doing here? (*Left of door in hall.*)

MARTIN. (*Shoves his chair to Up Right, gives cup to* GIRL. *Up to door and Right of* BONIFACE. *Shaking his hand.*) Boniface! My dear friend! We were just talking about you!

GIRLS. Yes, that we were!

(MARTIN *pushes* BONIFACE *into room and follows.*)

BONIFACE. Well, that's always nice to hear. (*To* MARCELLE.) Well, and how are you, Mme. Cot?— (*Center of room.*) Actually I had a little business to do in this part of town, and so I said to myself, "I *must* drop in and say 'Hello' to Mme. Cot!"

MARCELLE. (*As though amazed.*) But how sweet of you! What a delightful thought!

THE MARTINS. Oh, yes! Yes! Yes! Indeed it is!

MARTIN. But, look here, old man! Do you usually go out in your shirtsleeves?

BONIFACE. I had an enormous tear—in my coat—so I took it into a tailor's nearby to be seen to; and while I was waiting to have it done, I said to myself, "I must drop in and say 'Hello' to Mme. Cot!"

MARCELLE. But how nice of you!— How very, very nice!

THE MARTINS. Oh yes, how nice!— How really nice!

MARGUERITE. (*Handing him a cup.*) A cup of tea, M. Boniface?

BONIFACE. (*Sits Left.*) Tea!— Oh yes, thank you *so* much!

PAQUERETTE. (*Holdiing sugar bowl.*) Sugar, M. Boniface?

BONIFACE. (*Taking sugar.*) Thank you *so* much! (*Aside.*) I'm damned if I thought I was going to have tea here with the Martins!

PAQUERETTE. (*Giggling.*) What a sweet tooth you have, M. Boniface!

BONIFACE. (*Continuing to put sugar in the cup.*) Thank you *so* much!

MARTIN. (*Picks up chair and brings it down; sits. Drinking his tea.*) Well now—what's the news— What's new in Paris?

BONIFACE. (*Drinking his tea.*) Well—it's a Republic!

MARTIN. And all goes well with your dear wife, since this afternoon?

BONIFACE. Splendidly!— Splendidly!— And yours, too?

(GEORGES *starts down stairs with hot water bottle.*)

MARTIN. But you know perfectly well she's been dead for eight years!

BONIFACE. Of *course!* (*Stands.*) Of *course!* Believe me, I— Oh well, it can't be helped now! (*Sits.*)

MARCELLE. (*Aside.*) Will *nothing* budge them?

GEORGES. (*Entering No. 10.*) Sur! Here's your hot water bottle!

MARCELLE. (*Aside.*) That's done it!

BONIFACE. (*Snatching the bottle from* GEORGES, *burns himself.*) Ow!

MARTIN. (*Perplexed.*) Your bottle?

BONIFACE. Yes— Well, yes, as a matter of fact— You see, every time I come to this hotel I always order a hot water bottle! They're very well known here for their hot water bottles!— Very well known!— Didn't you know?— Well, my wife said to me, if ever you are passing by the Hotel Paradiso you *must* get me one of their hot water bottles!— Isn't that so, Mme. Cot?

MARCELLE. (*Embarrassed.*) Oh, yes!— Yes!

GEORGES. What's that, sur?— But I never heard—

BONIFACE. (*Rises.*) Who spoke to you?— Be off!— Off!— Off! (*He pushes him to the door.*)

GEORGES. Eh?— Right you are, sur! (*He goes out, climbs the stairs and disappears Left.*)

BONIFACE. (*To* MARCELLE.) Well now, my dear lady, I can see that you are very tired— (*Almost in* MARTIN's *ear.*) tired!— I mustn't take up another instant of your time. So, if you will excuse me, I shall take my leave. (*Kisses her hand.*)

MARTIN. (*Getting up.*) You're tired? Oh, but you should have said so. (*To his daughters.*) Come, children. Let's go back to our room— We mustn't outstay our welcome!

GIRLS. Good night, Mme. Cot!

(MARTIN *takes his chair and, followed by his daughters, each with a chair, moves towards the door. The* GIRLS *go out.*)

MARTIN. (*To* MARCELLE.) Au revoir, good lady, and good night!

BONIFACE. (*Pushing him on.*) Yes, yes, let's go!

(MARTIN *backs out; followed by* BONIFACE. *Their chairs get entangled.*)

mind!— *Mind!* (*Whispering to* MARCELLE.) I'll go to put them off the scent and come straight back!—

MARCELLE. (*Shutting her door.*) Oh!— I'll never get over this!— Never!

MARTIN. (*Shaking* BONIFACE's *hand.*) Au revoir, my dear Boniface. Don't forget to give my best wishes to Mme. Boniface!

BONIFACE. (*Giving* MARTIN *the other chair, and shaking his hand.*) Oh, I won't forget!— I won't forget! (*As he goes.*) Oh dear! Oh dear! Oh dear! (*He goes upstairs and off Right.*)

(MARTIN *puts one of the chairs down. Going into the room, No. 11.*)

MARCELLE. (*Alone.*) Oh, no, no, no! Never again!— What a lesson— (*Picks up cup.*) Lord, what a lesson!

THE GIRLS. (*Embracing their father.*) Good night,
Pappa!

PERVENCHE. We're going to go and undress!

MARTIN. That's right! Your bathroom's over there.
(*The* GIRLS *move towards it. Go into it.*)
Not so much noise, please!— There are people sleeping!

MARCELLE. (*Pacing up and down; to herself.*) I can't
bear another minute in this beastly hotel!— As soon as
Boniface returns— (*She puts on her coat.*)

MARTIN. (*Stretching.*) Oh, it'll be good to get into
bed!

MARCELLE. Where is my hat!— (*At bed.*) Where is my
hat! (*To Down Center. She searches everywhere.*)

MARTIN. When one's been walking around all day!

MARCELLE. Perhaps I pushed it in there with *his*
things! (*She goes into the bathroom with a lighted
candle in her hand. The* LIGHTS *fade in room, Left.*)

MARTIN. (*Looking around his room. He catches sight
of Cot's toilet case. Combs his hair.*) Oh well!— I think
I'll smoke a cigar before turning in!— (*He takes a
minute cigar from his pocket.*) These don't look much
but they're not a bad smoke for ten sous! (*He notices
the box of cigars on the table.*) Hello!— What have we
here—a whole box!— (*Reading the trade mark.*) Prega-
lias, six francs twenty!— (*He puts his own back in his
pocket.*) This is really a most exceptional hotel!— Help
yourself to cigars!— And all for twenty francs a day!
(*He pockets the entire top layer and lights one of them.*)
This is really magnificent!

MARCELLE. (*Coming out of the bathroom.*) This place
is bewitched! My hat has simply *disappeared!*

(MARTIN, *smoking and taking up the candle-holder
in which the candle is flickering out.*)
(*Searching still; puts candle on bed table.*) Oh, that Boniface! Where *is* he?— What can he be up to? (*She opens
the door ajar and puts her face through.*)

MARTIN. (*Seeing the nightshirt on the bed in alcove.*)
And a nightshirt!— A nightshirt!— *And* slippers!—

They really think of everything! What more could one ask!

(BONIFACE *appears on the landing, carrying a hot water bottle under his arm.*)

MARCELLE. (*Peeping outside the door.*) Ah—there you are!— Come in!— Quickly!— Quickly!

BONIFACE. (*With a soft voice; on his toes; circumspect.*) Coming! Coming! (*Starts downstairs.*)

MARTIN. There's only one more thing I need—a hot water bottle— I must call the boy to get one!

MARCELLE. (*To* BONIFACE.) Hurry!— Hurry!

(MARTIN *appears in the hallway, with the candleholder in his hand. The* LIGHTS *fade in room Left.*) Oh! (*Shuts door quickly.*)

BONIFACE. Oh! (*He stands there stupefied.*)

MARTIN. Oh?— It's you!

BONIFACE. Well— Yes!— As a matter of fact— I came back especially to see you! I wanted to tell you something!—

MARTIN. (*Crosses Downstage.*) What? (*He puts down candle-holder.*)

BONIFACE. (*Crosses Downstage. Without conviction.*) Well—you know what I mean?

MARTIN. —Not exactly!

BONIFACE. Well, I was downstairs—and I heard some people talking—and they—were saying that frankly— they said that the government is within an inch of falling!

MARTIN. Well! Well! Well!

BONIFACE. What are we coming to? Merciful heaven! — Where are we all heading? (*A step Right.*) So I said to myself, Martin must be informed of this— So I instantly—

MARTIN. But how does it concern me?

BONIFACE. But do the affairs of the nation mean nothing to you? Well, then, I must be off! I must bid you good-night!— (*He moves to the stairs.*)

MARTIN. (*Perking up.*) Well, good-night!— And thanks all the same!

BONIFACE. Not at all!— Not at all!— Back you go to your room!— You mustn't catch cold!— Back you go!

MARTIN. I am waiting for the boy to ask him for a hot water bottle!— You said they were so good here!

BONIFACE. A hot water bottle! Here, take mine—do take mine! (*He hands it to* MARTIN.)

MARTIN. No, no!— My dear sir, I wouldn't dream of depriving you!—

BONIFACE. Not at all, my dear fellow— It's not depriving me. (*Aside.*) It's cold by now, anyway. (*Aloud.*) I can get another one downstairs as I leave!

MARTIN. Are you sure?— Well, it's extremely kind of you!

BONIFACE. It's nothing!— Nothing at all!— Now back you go! (*He points to room, No. 11.*)

MARTIN. Very well, then! Good-night!— (*He remains standing there in the doorway, smoking his cigar.*)

BONIFACE. (*Waiting for* MARTIN *to go.*) Good-night! (*Going upstairs to middle.*) Good-night!

MARTIN. (*With a little wave.*) Good-night!

BONIFACE. Good-night— (*He turns.*) Were you waiting for something?

(MARTIN *smiles and shakes his head.*)

(*With a forced smile.*) Well then, good-night! (*He disappears Right.*)

MARTIN. (*Returning to the bedroom.*) An enchanting character—enchanting! Oh!— I've forgotten the candle. (*He returns through the door to the hallway and comes face to face with* BONIFACE *who has returned.*) Oh, it's you again?

BONIFACE. (*Very out of countenance.*) Yes!— We never shook hands! (*He does so and runs back upstairs.*)

(MARTIN, *rather astonished, returns to his room.* BONI-
FACE *darts back and into Marcelle's room.*)

MARTIN. Well, I'd better get undressed! (*He goes
into his bathroom and the* LIGHTS *fade.*)

BONIFACE. Whew!

MARCELLE. At last! I thought you were never coming!

BONIFACE. But my dear, I had to get rid of all those
Martins, and you needn't think that that was so easy.

MARCELLE. Don't even speak of them!

BONIFACE. But would you believe it?— How did they
come to choose this one hotel when there are so many
others!— Pure bad luck!

MARCELLE. I should think it was!— Anyway, put on
your hat and coat, and let's get out of here! (*Goes Up
to bed to get stole.*)

BONIFACE. My hat and coat? Where are they?

MARCELLE. There!— In the bathroom. (*She points to
it.*)

BONIFACE. Oh! Very well—very well. (*He goes into
the bathroom.*)

MARCELLE. Oh, incidentally, what have you done with
my hat?

BONIFACE. (*Coming out, and putting his coat on.*)
What do you mean? Done with your hat? (*Getting
panicky; looks under table fringe.*) Oh!— Wait now!—
I remember I had it in my hand when I went upstairs
for air! I must have left it there! (*He giggles in embarrassment.*)

MARCELLE. (*Furious.*) So you left it upstairs? That
was really clever of you! What did you have to take it
up there for in the first place? You'd better run up and
get it right away! I'll wait for you!

BONIFACE. Yes, yes, wait for me!

MARCELLE. Well, off you go!—and hurry! Now I've
had *all* I can take! All—*and* more!

BONIFACE. (*Running out and bumping into AN-
NIELLO.*) Oh!

ANNIELLO. Oh! And vere are *you* off to?

BONIFACE. (*Running upstairs.*) I know where! I know where! (*He disappears aloft.*)

ANNIELLO. (*Amazed.*) Well, I'm very 'appy to 'ear it! (MARCELLE *goes into the bathroom.*)

(*Hearing the* BELL *ring.*) Now what? More customers? (*He sees* COT *coming up the stairs Left.*) Oh, it's da Signor expert! (*Comes downstairs and lights candle.*)

COT. (*Coming into view.*) Yes, it's me! (*He comes down to* ANNIELLO.)

ANNIELLO. And is Signor expert going to 'is bed?

COT. And has Signor Ghost made his appearance yet?

ANNIELLO. (*Giving him his candle.*) Not to da best of ma knowledge, Signor expert! (*He pushes door No. 11 open.*)

COT. How disappointing!

(*Crosses below* ANNIELLO *into room. The* LIGHTS *come up there.*)

ANNIELLO. Dat's right, Signor Know-it-all! (*He follows* COT *in.*)

COT. (*Puts candle on table. Seeing his box of cigars open.*) Hello!— What's been happening to my cigars?

ANNIELLO. What is dat, Signor expert?

COT. I said, my cigars!— This box was full a short time ago and now half of them are gone!— And where, may I ask?

ANNIELLO. Dat I do not know!

(BOTH *stand above table.*)

COT. So! *That* you do not know!— Well, they can't have gone out of their own accord!

ANNIELLO. I tink I see da light! It's da ghosts!!

COT. What? Cigar-smoking ghosts!

ANNIELLO. And why not?— Maybe the ghost like cigars.

Cot. Yes, I'm beginning to see only too clearly the type of ghosts you have here— Some thieving rogue who passes himself off as a phantom! (*Goes Up.*) All right, you may go now! Tomorrow I shall get to the bottom of this—*with* your employer!

Anniello. Dat is good, sir! Good-a night, Signor! 'Appy dreams, Signor!

Cot. Good-night to you!

Anniello. (*Crossing on to the landing; to front.*) I 'ope da ghosts will beat da 'ell out of 'im! (*He goes down the stairs Left.*)

Cot. There's a thief at large here!— Not a doubt of it!— A common thief! (*Looking at his brushes; putting them back in his case.*)

Boniface. (Boniface *appears coming down the stairs.*) Not a sign!— Not a sign!— I've looked everywhere— What can have happened to that damned hat!

Cot. (*Looking at the bed.*) And my nightshirt?—and my slippers?— So they've stolen those, too! (*He hangs up his hat.*)

Boniface. (*On the landing.*) Oh, she'll make a terrible scene— Well, it can't be helped— It's got to be faced! (*He enters room No. 10.*)

Cot. (*To himself.*) Do you know, I think I shall go to bed with my clothes on tonight—then if anything happens I shall be ready for action! (*Hat on chair Right. He stretches himself out on the alcove bed and starts to read.*)

Marcelle. (*Coming from bathroom.*) Well—where is it?

Boniface. (*Dramatic.*) Marcelle—please be brave!

Marcelle. Why?

Boniface. It's not there!— Someone's taken it!

Marcelle. Who?

Boniface. (*Simple.*) He didn't leave his name!

Marcelle. Charming!— Well, thank goodness I have this lace scarf to put over my head. (*She does so.*) Let's leave at once!

BONIFACE. Yes! I've had quite enough of this! (*Goes out to stairs.*)

MARCELLE. And so have I!— And what a lesson!— (*She goes upstairs after* BONIFACE.) What a lesson!

(*They vanish Down Left.*)

COT. (*With a yawn.*) Oh! I'm dead beat! Oh well!— out with the light! (*He blows the candle out, pulls curtains closed.*) Now for some sleep!

(MARCELLE *runs in Left, followed by* BONIFACE.)

MARCELLE. Heaven help us!— It's Victoire with my nephew Maxime!
(MARCELLE *into room No. 10;* BONIFACE *follows.*) Lock the door!

BONIFACE. The key!— Where is the key?— (*He suddenly points to the bathroom.*) There!— In there!— There's a bolt— Quickly— We must hide!

MARCELLE. (*Dashing into bathroom;* BONIFACE *first; she follows.*) What a night!— What a *night!*

(COT *is asleep in Room No. 11.* MAXIME *and* VICTOIRE *appear Left with* GEORGES *on the landing.* VICTOIRE *is carrying books and* MAXIME *a satchel.*)

GEORGES. This way, sur!— This way!

VICTOIRE. Come on, ducks!

MAXIME. (*Earnestly, to* VICTOIRE.) Victoire—Victoire— I do hope you realize the importance of the step we are about to take!

VICTOIRE. Oh yes!

GEORGES. (*Ogling and aping* ANNIELLO.) Oi can guess exactly the gennleman's requirements—a cosy little nest where the pretty loidy'll be at ease, eh?— She's a peach, sur!—a reg'lar peach!

MAXIME. (*Seriously enquiring.*) Do you *really* think so?

GEORGES. Oi suggest number noine! This 'ere is where the Princess of Poland spent her 'oneymoon with 'er Lord Chamberlin!

VICTOIRE. The room of a real Princess?!

GEORGES. Oh yes, Madame, you're in a very revoined hotel!

VICTOIRE. Oh, I *know!*— I've read them circulars!— Well, here we are— Let's take Number Nine, shall we?

GEORGES. That's the one for you, Madame, the very one. Well, now, if the lady and gentleman would like to see their room— (*He looks at them and chuckles. Gets candle and goes to No. 9.*)

MAXIME. (*Moved and tragic.*) He's laughing!— Laughing in our faces!

VICTOIRE. (*Dismissing it.*) Oh well, let him!!

(VICTOIRE *pulls at* MAXIME'S *arm.*)

MAXIME. (*Left of* VICTOIRE.) Wait! Victoire—wait! — I'm not at all sure where all this is leading!

VICTOIRE. Trust me! I'll give you Spinoza!

(GEORGES *follows them in— The lights fade on the landing. In room No. 11,* COT *is fast asleep. The* GIRLS *emerge from their bathroom. One carries a candle.*)

PAQUERETTE. (*Putting her candle on the bedside table.*) Bed at last!— And about time! (*She sits.*)

MARGUERITE. I bags this bed!

VIOLETTE. I bags this one!

PERVENCHE. No, that's mine! I got here first, I'm staying here!

VIOLETTE. It isn't! It isn't! You leave that bed alone!

(*Girlish altercation.*)

PAQUERETTE. (*Whispering.*) Not so much noise!—
Hush!— You heard what Pappa said!
> (*They all sit on the beds and take off their stockings.*)

Oh, I'm longing to get between the sheets! (*She gets into bed.*) Br-r-r! It's freezing!

(VIOLETTE *unpins her hair.*)

MARGUERITE. (*Carrying her bag and coming downstage.*) I'm going to use my curling irons before getting into bed.
VIOLETTE. Top marks! So shall I!
ALL. Yes, yes—curly curlers!
GEORGES. (*Coming out of No. 9.*) Good-night, sur!—
Nighty-night, Miss! (GEORGES *disappears downstairs Left.*)
GIRLS. Pass me the candle!— Me too!— Me too!

(*They squabble over the candle which goes out. The room and the landing are now in darkness.*)

PAQUERETTE. Now you've dropped it on the floor!
VIOLETTE. Butter-fingers!
MARGUERITE. I say, let's light the burners for our curling irons!

(*Sounds of whispering and searching. A match is lit and it is used to light their little blue night-lights, one after the other. The GIRLS are in a circle and their faces, as they bend over, are now faintly illuminated by a blue light.*)

PAQUERETTE. Look!— We're will o' the wisps!
VIOLETTE. (*Standing on her bed.*) We look like ghosts!
PERVENCHE. Yes! Yes! It reminds me of the Witches Song! (*They all stand on their beds and sing a Witch Song.*)

ALL. (*Singing.*)

> The witches on their brooms,
> They cackle as they fly—Hurrah!
> Dizzy with the dooms,
> They're hatching in their hide-aways
> They'll tiptoe to the cave
> Where still their cauldron steams and blows
> And into it they'll throw
> Elephants' ears and children's toes,
> Knee-caps, gnats and fly-blown cream.
> Bubbly, bubbly, bub,
> Oh, what a hectic scene.

COT. (*Sitting up in bed, petrified. Puts on hat.*) A-a-h! Spirits!— Ghosts!

(*The* GIRLS *have now jumped down and are dancing round the table, singing The Witches Song.*)
(*Jumping out of bed, his hands in the air.*) Daughters of Satan—avant! Help!

GIRLS. (*Seeing him.*) O-oh! (*They flee into their father's bathroom.*)

COT. Ghosts!— (*He rushes out to the hallway.*) Help!— Help!

VICTOIRE. (*Rushing from room No. 9, followed by* MAXIME.) What's the to-do? What's up?

COT. (*Shouting.*) Help!— Help! (*At bottom of stairs.*)

VICTOIRE. (*Face to face with* COT.) Monsieur Cot!

MAXIME. (*Behind.*) Uncle!

(MAXIME *rushes back into No. 9 and* VICTOIRE, *to hide, rushes into No. 11, and hides behind the curtains of the bed.*)

COT. (*Running upstairs, shouting.*) Spirits!— Spectres!— Phantoms!— Help!

MARTIN. (MARTIN *comes out of his bathroom with a lighted candle.*) Now what *is* all this nonsense you're telling me?— A man?— Where's there a man?— In the

bed, you say? (*He opens the curtains and sees* VIC-
TOIRE.)

VICTOIRE. Oh!

MARTIN. Oh, Madame!— I beg your pardon! (*Chuck-
ing.*) So that's what they call a man!— It's a woman!
(*He goes back to the bathroom, leaving the door open.*)
Children, you're talking nonsense!— It's not a man!—
It's a woman! (*He shuts the bathroom door and the
lights fade in room.*)

GIRLS' VOICES. (*Off.*) Yes! Yes! Pappa!— It's a man!

MAXIME. (*Coming out of No. 9.*) My uncle's gone!—
What *is* Victoire doing in that room? (*Enters room No.
11.*) There's no one here! (*Calling.*) Victoire! Victoire!

VICTOIRE. (*Emerging from the curtains.*) Psst!— Over
here!

(MARTIN *comes out of the bathroom followed by* GIRLS.
As the door opens, MAXIME *and* VICTOIRE *rush
behind the curtains.*)

MAXIME *and* VICTOIRE. Oh!

MARTIN. Very well, children, come and see for yourselves!

PAQUERETTE. Pappa, we saw him quite clearly— Cross
my heart!— It was a man!

MARTIN. I can see quite clearly, too— I certainly
know one sex from the other!

(VICTOIRE *rushes out from behind the curtains to
hallway and up to landing.*)

Look!— There!— What did I tell you? —It's a woman!

(MAXIME *rushes out.*)

GIRLS. No! No! Pappa— Look!— It's a man!!

MARTIN. (*Dumbfounded.*) A man *and* a woman!

MAXIME. (*On the landing, to* VICTOIRE.) Let's get
out!

VICTOIRE. Yes!— Yes!— Let's go!

(*They disappear down the stairs Left.*)

MARTIN. We must get to the bottom of this! (*Going to the doorway and calling.*) Boy! Boy!

GEORGES. (*Coming down the stairs from No. 9.*) What's up there?— What's all this din about?

MARTIN. Listen, boy, what's the meaning of all this? Finding men and women in our beds and the Lord knows what else!

GEORGES. 'S'truth, sur—really?— So you've seen them?

MARTIN. Seen?— Whom?

GEORGES. Well, Oi didn't like to tell you, sur—but the room is 'aunted!

THE MARTINS. Haunted!

(COT *appears, above, creeping downstairs.*)

GIRLS. (*With girlish cries, losing their heads.*) Ghosts! — Ghosts!— Oh!— Oh!—

(*They fly up the stairs, screaming, and terrify* COT, *who turns around and precedes them upstairs again and off Left.*)

MARTIN. (*Following his daughters.*) Children! Children! Heavens! Now they're rushing about the hotel in their shifts!

(BONIFACE *comes out of bathroom.*)

(*Calling as he goes.*) Children! Children! (*He disappears.*)

GEORGES. (*Following him up.*) —What an 'urly burly!—

(BONIFACE, *followed by* MARCELLE, *is seen coming out of the bathroom.*)

BONIFACE. (*To Down Left.*) What's going on?— What were all those shouts and strange noises?

MARCELLE. (*To Right of him.*) I know something awful is happening in this house!— I shall die of fright if we don't get out this minute!

BONIFACE. Yes!— Yes!— But wait!— We must be careful! (*He half opens the door and peeps through.*)

MARCELLE. (*Going up behind him.*) I shan't be able to breathe until I'm out of this place!

(COT *reappears, starts downstairs.*)

BONIFACE. (*Looking round the hallway.*) Not a soul! You go first!

MARCELLE. (*Joining* BONIFACE.) Ah!—at last!

COT. (*Flying down the stairs, like a madman.*) Help!— Ghosts!— Ghosts!

MARCELLE. (*In terror.*) Heavens!— Back! (*She rushes back into room.*)

BONIFACE. (*Following her.*) What was it?

MARCELLE. My husband!

BONIFACE. (*In terror.*) Oh! (*He slams the door shut; he and* MARCELLE *take position holding door shut.*)

COT. (*Who has seen them without recognizing them.*) Human beings!— Thank heaven for that! (*Trying to open the door.*) Open the door!— Open the door! (*Knocking—pulling handle.*)

BONIFACE. (*The other side.*) You can't come in!— You can't come in!

COT. Yes, yes, for pity's sake open the door!

MARCELLE. (*To* BONIFACE.) Don't let him in!

BONIFACE. It's no good!— I can't hold out any longer!— He's stronger than I am!

COT. Please! Please! Let me in! Let me in!

(*The door gives way and* COT *lunges in.* BONIFACE *is hurtled back to the fireplace, into which he disappears to hide.* MARCELLE *grabs* COT'S *top-hat which she pushes down over her head, down to her neck.*)

That's my hat, Madame! Give it to me!— Give it to me! (*He tries to take it off her head.*)

MARCELLE. (*Hanging on to the brim, and screaming.*) Help!— Help!— Help!

(BONIFACE *comes out of the fireplace, his face blackened with soot.* BONIFACE *whirls* COT *round and gives him a gigantic push which hurtles him to the hallway.* BONIFACE *closes door.*)

COT. Oh!— Poltergeists!— Fighting mad!— Phantoms!— Spirits!— Ghosts!— Help!— Help!— Help!— (*He rushes upstairs and off Left.*)

BONIFACE. It's all right, Marcelle!— He's gone!

MARCELLE. (*Taking the hat off her face, putting it on table.*) At last!— Oh, what an experience!— What an— (*She sees* BONIFACE *and screams; falls back.*) A-a-h!—

BONIFACE. No, no!— It's me!— Boniface!

MARCELLE. (*Almost fainting.*) Oh, Boniface—this night will be the death of me! Good gracious, but you're pitch black!

BONIFACE. Yes, yes! Take no notice! (*Moves away.*)

MARCELLE. Merciful heaven, what we've been through!

BONIFACE. Well, thank heavens, it's over!— Now we can catch our breath!

MARCELLE. Yes, thank the Lord! What a relief!

BONIFACE. Yes—it's all over!— Thank goodness!

(WHISTLES, *off-stage.*)

What's that?

MARCELLE. Not again!— No, no!— Not again!

ANNIELLO. (*Entering Right on landing.*) Madonna Mia!— Evvabody run for eet! (*To door of room No. 10.*) Da Dicks! (*Knocking.*)

BONIFACE. Da Dicks!

ANNIELLO. (*Knocking on door.*) Da dicks is here!!

MARCELLE. What's he saying?

BONIFACE. The Dicks!— We're lost!— It's the Police!

MARCELLE. The Police!— Quick, we must escape!

(*They rush out to the hallway. The* INSPECTOR OF POLICE *runs in Right upstairs, followed by his men.*)

MARCELLE. (*Seeing him.*) Oh! A Police Inspector! (*She rushes back into her room and slams the door.*)

BONIFACE. Let me in! Let me in!

INSPECTOR. (*Seeing her.*) Ah— Ah! (*Pointing to* BONIFACE.) Arrest that man!

BONIFACE. (*Struggling.*) Me?— But, gentlemen! I protest—

POLICEMAN. Yes, yes. All in good time!

INSPECTOR. (*Pointing to the door No. 10.*) In there, you!

(*The* POLICEMAN *tries to open the door.*)

MARCELLE. (*Leaning against the other side of the door.*) You can't come in! You can't come in!

INSPECTOR. Break in!

(*The door gives way to the* POLICEMAN, *who enters.*)

MARCELLE. Oh!— I'm lost!

POLICEMAN. Come along, Miss.

BONIFACE. (*Held by the* POLICEMAN.) Oh, the poor soul!

MARCELLE. (*Going out to the hallway.*) Heavens above!

INSPECTOR. (*To* MARCELLE.) Step forward, please, Madame!

MARCELLE. But, Inspector, what have I done? I am an honest woman! (*Turns and to Down Right.*)

BONIFACE. Yes, yes!— It's true, Inspector— This lady is an honest woman!

INSPECTOR. (*To* MARCELLE.) So much the better for you! (*To a* POLICEMAN.) Take that gentleman in there! (*He points to room No. 10.*)

BONIFACE. (*Resisting.*) But look here!— Look here!

POLICEMAN. Come along now!— No answering back! (*He takes* BONIFACE *into room.*)

INSPECTOR. (*To* MARCELLE.) Now, Madame, you first —and mind, no lying!— Kindly tell me your name!

MARCELLE. I don't know what you mean, Inspector!— I am here with my husband.

INSPECTOR. (*Shrugging his shoulders.*) Indeed!

MARCELLE. Certainly! I am the wife of Monsieur—of the gentleman you have just taken in there!

INSPECTOR. (*Skeptical.*) Of course, Madame, of course — And would it be indiscreet to enquire your name?

MARCELLE. But Inspector— (*Aside.*) There's nothing else for it! (*To* INSPECTOR.) My name is Mme. Boniface!

INSPECTOR. Very good! (*To* POLICEMAN.) Bring in the person who is in there. (*Points Right.*)

POLICEMAN. (*In the doorway.*) You there!— This way!

INSPECTOR. (*To* BONIFACE.) And now you, Monsieur! What is your name?

BONIFACE. (*To the* INSPECTOR, *with aplomb.*) Inspector, I really don't know what you mean! My conduct is beyond reproach— That lady is my wife!

MARCELLE. (*A gleam of hope.*) Oh!

INSPECTOR. And your name?

BONIFACE. M. Cot!

MARCELLE. Oh, no!

(WHISTLES *and* SCREAMS, *off.*)

MARTIN. Children! Children!

(ANNIELLO, GEORGES, MARTIN *and his four* DAUGH-
    TERS, *appear coming down the stairs, followed by*
    POLICEMAN.)

INSPECTOR. (*To the* POLICE.) Stop! Arrest all these people and take them off to the police station!

ALL. The *police station?*

(*Confusion, cries, protestations, struggles.*)

CURTAIN

END OF ACT TWO

ACT THREE

Same as Act One.

(*At the rise of the Curtain, the room is empty and the window is open as it was at the end of Act One. The clock is striking seven.*)

(BONIFACE *appears at the window; his face is still quite black. He climbs over the window-sill, and having pulled up his rope ladder after him, he tiptoes over to the door Left, to make sure that it is still locked. Then he goes over to the fire chest and puts the rope ladder away in it. He quickly takes off his jacket, his waistcoat and his hat, and carries them into his bedroom, Right. He re-enters immediately, in a smoking jacket. He takes a scarf from one of the pockets which he puts round his neck. He then comes downstage and gives the audience a look of satisfaction.*)

BONIFACE. She hasn't returned! She must have spent the night at her sister's. Good! Now I'm ready for her. (*To Down Center.*) I defy anyone to give a single reason why my wife should throw me so much as a suspicious glance. This is exactly how she has seen me every morning for twenty years—but what a night! *What* a night! (*Gestures to audience; turns Right and starts Up.*)
        (*A* KNOCK *at the door Up Left.*)
        (*Aside. To Right Center above sofa.*) That can't be her already? Anyway, she has the key— She wouldn't knock. (*Aloud.*) Who is it?
        VICTOIRE. (*Behind door.*) It's me, monsieur!— It's Victoire!
        BONIFACE. (*Moves a few steps to Center. Aside.*) Vic-

87

toire—oh, she's a wicked one!— I'd like to know how she explains her presence in the Hotel Paradiso last night! But if I open my mouth, I'm in the soup! (*Aloud.*) What do you want?

VICTOIRE. Your coffee, Monsieur!

BONIFACE. All right— Bring it in!

VICTOIRE. I can't— I haven't the key!

BONIFACE. Well, go and ask Mme. Boniface—*she's* got it! (*Smiles to himself.*)

VICTOIRE. She's not back yet, Monsieur!

BONIFACE. Not back?— Oh! Her sister's condition must be extremely critical!

VICTOIRE. Well, what shall I do, Monsieur?

BONIFACE. Well, I don't know— I haven't the key! You'd better wait until Madame gets back!

VICTOIRE. Very well, Monsieur!

BONIFACE. (*Crosses to Left end of sofa; picks key up off floor and holds key in hand. Aside.*) My key! But then if I unlock the door—bang goes my alibi!— What a *night!*— Raided and rounded up like a lot of bandits! (*He sits on the sofa.*)

(KNOCK *on the door Up Left.*)
Who is it?

MARCELLE. (*Behind door, in a low voice.*) Boniface!— It's me!

BONIFACE. What do you mean, *me?* Who's me?

MARCELLE. *Me!*— Marcelle!

BONIFACE. (*Rises and to door Up Left; stops suddenly.*) Are you alone?

MARCELLE. Yes, yes!— Open the door!

BONIFACE. All right! (*Opening it.*) Draw the bolt on your side!

MARCELLE. There!— I have! (*Enters.*) Oh, Boniface! Boniface! (*Crosses to Down Right below sofa to Up Right of sofa.*)

BONIFACE. (*He locks the door again.*) Oh Marcelle, what a night!— What a night! (*Crosses Center.*)

MARCELLE. I'm ruined!— Done for!— And all because

of you! (*She walks away in a flurry of agitation; over to Right Center.*)

BONIFACE. (*Following her.*) No, no, you mustn't think that!— Not for an instant!— It's not as bad as all that!— What if we *were* caught in a hotel together— After all, we're not rogues or vagabonds—that's all the police are after—rogues and vagabonds!

MARCELLE. (*Over to* BONIFACE.) It's not that— You know these police— Once they get their hands on you there are investigations, enquiries, papers to sign—forms to fill in—and if one of them should fall into my husband's hands, the cat will be out of the bag! Oh, Boniface! Boniface!— What's to become of us? (*Crosses to below sofa and faces front.*)

BONIFACE. (*Crosses to Left of* MARCELLE; *kneeling before her.*) Come now, courage!— Courage!— (*Takes Marcelle's hands; kisses her.*) What a timid little rabbit!— What a frightened little pussy! (*Rises; change of tone.*) You've something black on your nose!

MARCELLE. Something black?— Me?— Well, what about you? (*Leading him to the mirror.*) Have a look at your *own* face?

BONIFACE. *Me?* (*Looking at himself in the mirror.*) Good gracious me!— It's all that soot from last night! Ah! One trial after another! (*Runs up to trestle table and picks up napkin and water jug and starts to clean face.*)

(*They wipe their faces with the aid of a napkin and water from the water-jug.*)

MARCELLE. (*Rises and to mirror Down Right.*) Ah, you've said it! What a night, *indeed! What* a night! (*Crosses Up to Right of* BONIFACE. *Change of tone.*) After you with the jug! (*Snatches jug from* BONIFACE— *to Left end of sofa and sits.*)

BONIFACE. Yes, it certainly was a night!— (*Crosses to Left of* MARCELLE *and takes jug.*) But it really could

have been much worse— We might have had to spend
the night in the Police Station, like the others— At least
the Inspector showed his confidence in us by releasing us
for the time being!

MARCELLE. But of course! Because he realized immediately with whom he was dealing!

BONIFACE. (*Cleaning face with napkin.*) Yes! *And*
because I paid him twenty thousand francs' bail! (*Pointing to his face.*) All gone?

MARCELLE. (*Tugs at his coat and* BONIFACE *stops.*)
No!

(BONIFACE *crosses below her to Center of sofa.*)
You paid him twenty thousand francs!

BONIFACE. I certainly did! I gave him the choice
between my word of honour as a gentleman and twenty
thousand francs' bail. He settled for the twenty thousand
francs!— (*Crosses to desk Down Right and peers in
mirror.*) On condition that I bring along your identity
papers this afternoon.

MARCELLE. There you are! And as you'll never be able
to produce papers proving that you are M. Cot—what is
going to happen? If the Inspector doesn't get the papers,
he'll come straight here!

BONIFACE. (*Still dabbing at his face.*) Come here?
He'll never do that!— In any case I intend to pay a
personal visit to the President of the Senate himself. (*To
commode with water pitcher and placing it there with
napkin.*)

MARCELLE. The President of the Senate? (*Rising and
retreating a step.*)

BONIFACE. Certainly. Already, last night while you
were calmly returning to your home, *I*— (*Steps Left.*)

MARCELLE. (*Laughing bitterly.*) Calmly!— Calmly!
(*Moves Up a step.*) Oh, I like that!

BONIFACE. Well, all right then—*not* calmly— I was
actually there!—at the home of the President of the
Senate.

MARCELLE. And you saw him?

BONIFACE. No! He was out—at a ball— (*Crosses to Right of* MARCELLE.) But a fig for that!

(MARCELLE *walks Down Left.*)

I shall call on him again later on— He's my personal friend— I shall tell him the whole truth. (*Crosses Left to below sofa.*)

MARCELLE. (*Crosses below sofa to Right end of sofa.*) Oh, I shall never be able to look him in the face!

BONIFACE. Well, nobody is going to ask you to, my dear—

MARCELLE. Oh! (*Crosses to Left end of sofa.*)

BONIFACE. I shall merely tell him that the honor of a lady is at stake—and he will hush the whole thing up!

MARCELLE. (*Up to Right end of sofa.*) Do you really think so?

BONIFACE. I'm convinced of it!

MARCELLE. Oh, how much simpler (*Moves Up.*) it would have been if we hadn't allowed ourselves to get into this ridiculous situation in the first place!— (*To Right end of sofa.*) And what an absurd idea of yours to go and call yourself M. Cot, when your name is M. Boniface! (*Moves Down Right.*)

BONIFACE. (*To above Left end of sofa.*) Well, really! It was your fault— If you hadn't gone and called yourself Mme. Boniface, when your name is Mme, Cot!

MARCELLE. Excuse me! I said my name was Mme. Boniface so that they would think I was your wife!

BONIFACE. Yes, but I said my name was M. Cot so they would think I was your husband!

MARCELLE. But, my dear, you couldn't hope to make the Inspector believe your wife's name was Mme. Boniface when you had already said that your name was M. Cot!

BONIFACE.

(*He and* MARCELLE *slowly sit sofa.*)

But, my dear, how could I guess when I said that my name was M. Cot, that you had already said that your name was Mme. Boniface!

MARCELLE. (*Irritated; rises and crosses Down Right.*) Well, when you don't know—you should say nothing!

BONIFACE. (*Aside.*) Ah, ladies' logic!

(*A* KNOCK *at the door.*)

Who is it?

COT. (*Off stage.*) It's me, Cot!

(BONIFACE *rises and back to Right Center.*)

MARCELLE. (*Low voice.*) My husband! (*Above Right end sofa.*)

BONIFACE. (*Motioning her to keep quiet.*) Shush! (*To* COT, *through the door, tentatively.*) What do you want?

COT. (*Off-stage.*) I must have a word with you!

BONIFACE. (*Over to Up Left of door.*) I can't open the door— My wife has locked me in and gone off with the key!

COT. Oh, hell!

BONIFACE. Look—go round into the garden—take the gardener's ladder, and come in through the window!

COT. A good idea! All right, then! I'll go and get the ladder!

BONIFACE. Yes, do!

MARCELLE. (*Crosses to Right of* BONIFACE.) *Now!*— Let me out!

BONIFACE. (*Listening.*) Wait!— I can still hear his footsteps— Ssh! He's down the stairs! (*Runs Up to window.*) You can slip across now!

(*Takes key from pocket and runs to Up Left door and unlocks it; moves* MARCELLE *below him and out door.*)

Don't forget to shoot the bolt!

MARCELLE. No, no!— Oh, what a night! What a *night!*

(*She goes out, and* BONIFACE *locks the door after her.*)

BONIFACE. (*Going back to the window, Left of trestle*

table.) What a morning! (*To* COT, *off-stage.*) Are you there?

COT. (*Appears above sill.*) Yes, yes!— Here I come!

BONIFACE. Careful now!— Don't fall off!

COT. (COT *climbs over the sill and to Right of trestle table. He has an enormous black eye. To below trestle table.*) Well—here we are! Oh, my friend, what a night I've had—*what* a night!

BONIFACE. What's happened to your eye?

COT.

(*Comes Down Right of trestle table;* BONIFACE *Left of it. Sitting.*) Oh, I'm in a pretty state, I can tell you!— You don't believe in ghosts, do you?

BONIFACE. No, I don't.

COT. Well, I didn't believe in them either! (*Rising.*) But, my friend, I'm afraid one *has* to believe in them from now on (*To above Right end of sofa.*)— *I* have actually seen them!—

BONIFACE. (*To Center, sits Left end of sofa.*) *You* have?

COT. Indubitably—and with my own eyes!

BONIFACE. (*Mocking.*) So you've met the bogeys face to face!

COT. (*Up Right end of sofa.*) I tell you I *have!*— I was as skeptical as you are— I breezed airily into that hotel, firmly convinced that any noises there were from a faulty water tank!— But not a bit of it—not a *bit* of it! I had only been asleep for about half an hour in this haunted chamber, when I woke up to find myself surrounded by wild will-o'-the-wisps, and supernatural voices, of an apparently feminine gender, dancing around me in a sort of frenzied saraband! As you can imagine, dignity and pride went to the winds, and I grabbed my bits and pieces and flew!— (*Moves Down Right.*) flew like a March hare!— Finally—in another room—I thought I espied two ordinary human beings!— And what a room that turned out to be!—*What* a room!

BONIFACE. (*Forgetting himself.*) Yes. Yes, Number Ten!

COT. Number Ten?— (*Turns toward sofa.*) What makes you think it was Number Ten particularly?

BONIFACE. (*Brought up short; rises and backs up a step.*) Eh?— Well, I don't know— Why shouldn't it be Number Ten?

COT. Well, Number Ten, then!— I rushed into it— (*To above Right end of sofa.*) and there was a woman— or at least something that bore a certain resemblance to a woman—with a dress with—um— (*He indicates bobbles and bits with his hands.*) —I couldn't see her face because it was buried under my hat.

BONIFACE. Under your *hat?*

COT. Yes, yes! Don't ask me why!— I didn't have time to take it all in! But that dress!— That dress! I'd recognize it in a million!

BONIFACE. You *wouldn't!*

COT. I certainly would!— And at that very moment— (*To front.*) I tell you it was black magic—out popped a chimney sweep from the fireplace! (*To* BONIFACE.) A chimney sweep—of about your build!

BONIFACE. (*Turning away quickly; sits chair by desk Up Left.*) Oh, no, no! *Much* taller! (*Pulls knees up.*)

COT. What do you mean—much taller?

BONIFACE. (*Befuddled.*) Well—you know what these chimney sweeps are!— They are always much, much taller!

COT. (*Up to trestle table.*) Possibly so!— I hadn't time to measure him! Anyway, before I had time to pull myself together he was upon me, and then— (*Front.*) Bong! I received a blow in the eye and a kick in the—

BONIFACE. (*Pointing.*) Kicked in the eye?

COT. No, no, no! That was the *blow!* Ah, (*Sits high stool.*) that hotel has seen the last of me, *I* can tell you! I only hope that *you* are never called upon to spend a night with poltergeists and fighting demons! (*M ps brow.*)

BONIFACE. (*Aside.*) He believes it! (*Aloud.*) And tell me, does your wife believe this story about the ghosts?

COT. My wife? I haven't even seen her yet! When I got back in the early hours I knocked on the door, but she didn't answer!

BONIFACE. She didn't answer?

COT. No! She must have been sleeping like a log! (*Rising.*) So I went and slept in the guest room.

(MAXIME'S *voice is heard in the garden, off-stage.*)

MAXIME. Uncle!— Uncle Henri!

COT. Good heavens! (*He goes Up Right of trestle table to window.*)

BONIFACE. (*Following him.*) That sounds like Maxime's voice.

COT. (*To* MAXIME, *off-stage.*) It does! It is! Maxime! What are you doing here? Why aren't you at school?

MAXIME. (*Off-stage.*) I'll explain it all in a minute. Uncle!

COT. Well, you'd better climb up the ladder, and explain!

(BONIFACE *sits on high stool.*)

MAXIME. (*Appearing at the window with a cigarette in his mouth; to Left of trestle table.*) Good *morning*, M. Boniface. Good *morning*, Uncle. Good Lord! What's happened to your eye?

COT. Er— Nothing!— Nothing at all!— (*Amazed.*) You're looking very bright and breezy this morning. Why aren't you at school? (*Goes to above sofa; pats pillow; to Left of sofa and below.*)

MAXIME. Well, I was just going to tell you— You see— I can't *think* how it happened—but—I must have forgotten to wind my watch yesterday morning— I'd got the time all wrong—and when I arrived at the college gates, I found everything bolted and barred! (*Sits on sofa.*)

COT. (*When* MAXIME *sits,* COT *crosses to above Left end of sofa.*) What's all this? (*Suspicious.*) There's something funny going on here!

MAXIME. Something funny!— Oh, Uncle! Really, you know me!

BONIFACE. (*Aside.*) !!!!

COT. (*Left.*) Well, why didn't you come straight back here?

MAXIME. Well, Uncle dear, it was so late—and as you weren't here yourself— I was anxious not to worry Auntie.

COT. Well, where did you spend the night, then?

MAXIME. At the Continental Hotel— You know the Continental, don't you? —Quite good!

COT. Are you quite *sure?*

MAXIME. Oh, Uncle!— *Really!* So you see, when I arrived this morning at the headmaster's office, he told me that I would have to get a note from you explaining my absence.

COT. Well, well! We'll see about that! (*Over to Right of* BONIFACE.)

MAXIME. (*Aside.*) Lucky the old buffer didn't recognize me last night!

MARCELLE. (*At the door, off-stage.*) Henri! Henri!

(BONIFACE *rises.*)

COT. There's my wife calling! (*To* MARCELLE, *through the Up Left door.*) Here I am, my dear!

MARCELLE. Well, open the door!

COT. I can't, it's locked!— And Mme. Boniface has the key— I had to come in through the window— I am here with Boniface!

MARCELLE. Oh!

BONIFACE. (*Crosses to Right of Up Left door; as if he hadn't seen her.*) Good day to you, Mme. Cot!

MARCELLE. (*Off.*) Good day to you, M. Boniface!

BONIFACE. (*Bowing to the door, as if he could see her.*) And how *are* you this morning? Did you sleep well?

MARCELLE. Oh, so, so! I had a rather restless night!

BONIFACE. (*Acting up.*) But you're in good spirits, I trust!

COT. Well, speaking of restless nights, *I'm* the one who really had one! Do you know what happened to me?

MARCELLE. No?

COT. Ah!— It was unbelievable— Do you know the Hotel Paradiso?

(MAXIME *Up*.)

MARCELLE. (*Off-stage.*) I've never heard of it! I've never even *heard* of it!

BONIFACE. No, we've never even heard of it! We've never even heard of it!

MAXIME. Neither have I! I've never even heard of it!

COT. (*Crosses toward* MAXIME.) Well, of *course* you've never heard of it!— It's an extremely shady establishment!— How *could* you have heard of it? (*Turns to* BONIFACE.)

BONIFACE. Yes! You're right there!

COT. Anyway, (*Crosses to Down Left.*) to get back to his hotel—but dammit!— It's very inconvenient talking through a locked door like this— Wait for me while I get out through the window and come round by the garden— I'll be with you in a minute.

MARCELLE. All right!

COT. (*To* BONIFACE; *bows.*) Will you excuse me? (*Crosses below* BONIFACE *to his Right.*) I parted on rather bad terms with my wife last night, so I'd like to take this opportunity to go and make it up! (*Bows; he goes to the window.*)

BONIFACE. Of course. I understand! (*Bows.*)

COT. (*Turns to* MAXIME.) Down you go! I'll follow you!

MAXIME. Right you are, Uncle!

(*Rising and Up Left of trestle table and out window.* BONIFACE *follows to Right of trestle.*)

COT. (*As his leg goes over the sill.*) Are you coming too?

BONIFACE. What me? Oh, no, no, no!— Certainly not. I shall stay here! (*Runs to above sofa; aside.*) Mustn't forget my alibi! (*Runs to door, unlocks it, and then runs back to the window, shouting.*) I say, take the ladder away from the wall, do you mind?— Yes, take it away!

COT. (*Off-stage.*) Right you are!

(BONIFACE *whistles and moves Down Left Center.*)

MARCELLE. (*Outside door.*) Has he gone?

BONIFACE. (*Running back to the door.*) Yes. Draw the bolt! (*Opening the door.*)

MARCELLE. (*At door.*) What did he say?

BONIFACE. (*He and she run to Down Left Center; he Right of* MARCELLE.) Nothing! It's all right— He doesn't suspect a thing!

MARCELLE. Thank goodness for that!

BONIFACE. (*Urgently.*) Only, for heaven's sake— That dress you were wearing last night— It was all he saw of you— It's the only clue he has— Tear it up! Burn it! Give it away! But whatever you do, never let him set eyes on it again!

MARCELLE. What a good thing you told me! I'll give it away immediately!

BONIFACE. (*Motions* MARCELLE *to the door.*) He may come up the stairs— Away with you! (*He shuts the door in her face.*) The bolt! Don't forget to shoot the bolt!

(*The* BOLT *is heard being shot.*)

(*Turns around with key and moves Up to high stool; sits swinging legs.*) Whew! Well, *that's* all right!! (*Sits down.*) But, d'you know, I'm getting rather fed up with being incarcerated in this room! (*Stands.*) What the blazes does she think she's doing, being away all this time?— I don't mind her sister being ill, but she might at least remember that I'm locked up in here!

VICTOIRE. (*Off-stage, at the door.*) Monsieur! Monsieur!

BONIFACE. Is that you, Victoire?

VICTOIRE. (*Off-stage.*) Yes, Monsieur.

BONIFACE. What is it?— What's the matter?

VICTOIRE. A telegram for you, M'sieu!

BONIFACE. (*Rises and Down to Up Left door.*) Eh?— Well, you'd better push it under the door!

VICTOIRE. Here it is, M'sieu! (*She slides it under the door.*)

BONIFACE. (*Taking up telegram.*) It must be from my wife. (*To Center, opening it.*) No, it's from her sister! (*Reading.*) "Very worried—expected Angelique for dinner—waited in vain. Is something wrong?— Please wire." —Well, well, *well!* (*Moves two steps Right.*) She didn't go to her sister's?— She certainly left here to go— Where?— *Where?* (*His face lights up.*) Perhaps she's been kidnapped on the road! No, no, I'm afraid the days of heroic deeds are past!— But then—what *can* it be? (*Crosses to below sofa and sits Left end.*) Don't tell me that *she*—that Mme. Boniface has been up to a trick or two! It's possible, but highly improbable—when one considers the lady—

ANGELIQUE. (*Behind door, off-stage, her voice fraught with emotion.*) Boniface!— Boniface!

BONIFACE. (*Rises and crosses to Center. Quietly.*) There she is! Turning up like a bad penny!

ANGELIQUE. Boniface!

BONIFACE. She sounds very excited! Well, off we go, to bed! (*He runs into his bedroom.*)

ANGELIQUE. (*Pulls open door; back to audience.*) Oh, Boniface!— Benedict! My dear! (*She swings to Right and faces front. She has an enormous black eye. She leans against door.*) Oh, what a night! *What* a night!

(*Moves down; taking off her coat.*) Benedict! (*Crosses to Center.*) Benedict! Where *are* you?

BONIFACE. (*Off-stage, yawning.*) Oh, hello there!

ANGELIQUE. It's I, my love! Your Angelique! Come here, quickly!

BONIFACE. (*Off-stage.*) What is it?

ANGELIQUE. I am only just *alive!* (*Steps toward Right.*)

BONIFACE. (*Off-stage.*) Good!

ANGELIQUE. (*Down to desk Right; takes off hat.*) Ah! Wait till he hears what happened to me! Wait till he hears how near to disaster I've been while he was sleeping peacefully in his bed! Benedict! (*Crosses below sofa to Up Center.*) Come quickly!

BONIFACE. (*Appearing at the bedroom door.*) Coming! Coming! (*Over to Right of* ANGELIQUE.)

ANGELIQUE. (*Puts hands on* BONIFACE'S *shoulders and leans; lowers head on* BONIFACE'S *Right arm.*) Ah! Benedict! I'm so happy to see you!

BONIFACE. There! There!— Me too!— (*Lifts* ANGELIQUE *up.*) But what's it all about?

ANGELIQUE. Oh, what a night! What a *night!*

BONIFACE. (*Aside.*) Those words are beginning to sound familiar! (*Taking her head between his hands.*) Angelique! Look at me! (*Turns her around—she steps away.*) Gracious heavens, what's happened to you?— You've got a black eye!

ANGELIQUE. (*Sits Left end of sofa.*) Oh, Boniface, Boniface! Do you realize, you very nearly lost me!

BONIFACE. (*Crosses to Left of* ANGELIQUE; *very calm.*) Is that so!

ANGELIQUE. Word of honour!

BONIFACE. (*Still calm.*) Really?

ANGELIQUE. Would you have minded, *terribly!*

BONIFACE. Naturally, my dear!

ANGELIQUE. Oh, my dear! I had an accident—a ghastly accident, which nearly deprived you of my person forever!

BONIFACE. (*Without conviction, crossing above sofa towards Right.*) Don't say that! You'll break my heart!

ANGELIQUE. (*Rises and follows.*) Oh! My own dear one! (*She presses him onto Right end of sofa.*)

BONIFACE. What's it all about?

ANGELIQUE. (*Retreats to Center and turns front.*) Well, as you know, I hired a carriage to take me to my sister's in Versailles. At first everything went well and there we were, trotting along, all three of us—

BONIFACE. All *three?*

ANGELIQUE. Yes, the driver, the horse and me! Suddenly, as we were going through the gates of Paris, a train whistle frightened the horse—and it bolted!

BONIFACE. Did it really?

ANGELIQUE. (*Center.*) The driver tried to rein him in! Impossible!— And there we were, flying, flying and hurtling through space—out into the countryside, and not a soul in sight to rescue us— (*To above* BONIFACE.) I tell you, Benedict, it's in moments like those—when life is threatened that a woman realizes what her husband means to her! Believe me, I thought of you every second — (*Straightens up.*) you, who weren't even in danger— And I said to myself— (*With emotion.*) I wish he were here too!

BONIFACE. Thank you, my dear!

ANGELIQUE. (*Crosses Center and turns.*) But unfortunately you weren't there! So what do you think I did?— I lost my head!— I opened the door and I leapt! And—landed—bong!—on a pile of rotten potatoes!

BONIFACE. Goodness gracious me!

ANGELIQUE. (*Crosses and sits Left end of sofa.*) After that I lost consciousness of everything! All I know is that I came to in the early hours of the morning, and found myself in a peasant's cottage, surrounded by strange people whom I didn't know from Adam, and who seemed glad to see that I was alive at all!— Such good people they were! I was sorry that I had only a thousand francs in my purse— I would gladly have given them everything we possess!

BONIFACE. Surely rather excessive?

ANGELIQUE. But they saved my life!

BONIFACE. That's what I was thinking!

ANGELIQUE. This morning, when they saw that I felt a little better, they fixed up a sort of vegetable cart and trundled me back to Paris, to the Etoile. There I took a cab—and here I am!

BONIFACE. (*Calm still.*) What a terrible thing!

ANGELIQUE. (*In tears.*) Boniface! When I think of it— it all comes back to me!— The horse! The rotten potatoes! Oh—your poor little wife! (*Sobs.*)

BONIFACE. There! There! Don't cry!

ANGELIQUE. Yes, but think!— Suppose you had lost me— What would you have done?

BONIFACE. (*With his arms around her.*) I would never have married again, my dear, I can promise you that!

VICTOIRE. (VICTOIRE *enters with letters. To Down Left.*) The post, Madame!

ANGELIQUE. (*Indicating sofa.*) All right.

BONIFACE. (*Rises; moves Right.*) Well, I had better get dressed! (*He enters the bedroom.*)

ANGELIQUE. Yes, do! Oh, I'm a mass of aches and pains! (*Lies on sofa, head Right.*) I must take a bath.

VICTOIRE. (*Puts mail on sofa. Seeing* ANGELIQUE'S *black eye.*) Oh Madame! You may not have noticed it, but your eye—it's as black as your hat!

ANGELIQUE. (*Outraged.*) Not noticed it? What do you mean, not noticed it!— *You'll* get your notice if you don't look out!— Go and prepare me a bath this instant!

VICTOIRE. Very well, Madame.

ANGELIQUE. And put some bran into it!

VICTOIRE. Yes, Madame. (*Turning.*) Oh, I'm sorry, Madame, there's no bran left—the donkey has eaten the lot!

ANGELIQUE. What have you got?

VICTOIRE. (*Center.*) Well, there's oats!

ANGELIQUE. I don't mean for the donkey, I mean for me!

VICTOIRE. Well, we have some starch—

ANGELIQUE. All right. then, put some starch in!

VICTOIRE. Very well, Madame. (*She goes out Left bedroom.*)

BONIFACE. (*Off-stage, singing.*) Oh Spring, give your fragrance of roses!

ANGELIQUE. (*Picking up the letters, reads.*) From the Inspector of Police. Now I wonder what *he* wants? (*Opens the envelope and reads.*) "Madame will kindly oblige by coming to my office on a matter which concerns her, and will kindly bring her identity papers." My identity papers?— What for? What do they mean? (*Continuing to read.*) "Mme. Boniface, who was caught in a police round-up last night—at the Hotel Paradiso, with M. Cott." (*Dumbfounded.*) But this is madness!— *Madness!* (*Distrait.*) I must have read it all wrong!— I must be getting delirious!

BONIFACE. (*In to above sofa, with a boot in his hand.*) My dear, there's a button missing off my boot!

ANGELIQUE. (*Turning to him and pulling him.*) Oh, my love!— You've come in just at the right moment!

BONIFACE. Why? What's the matter?

ANGELIQUE. (*Very upset.*) I think I must be going mad!— I must have forgotten how to read— Look at this! Oh no! It says—it says— No, it's too frightful! Read it! (*She gives him the letter.*)

BONIFACE. (*To Left Center; glancing at it; aside.*) What! The police!— Not *already!*

ANGELIQUE. Read it! Read it!

BONIFACE. (*Aside.*) This is catastrophic! (*Aloud, reading.*) "To Mme. Boniface, who was caught in a police round-up—at the Hotel Paradiso with M. Cot!"

ANGELIQUE. (*Rises to above sofa.*) Yes!— Me!— *Me!*— *I* was caught last night with M. Cot!

BONIFACE. (*Turns.*) You wretched creature—you admit it?

ANGELIQUE. (*Steps back.*) What?

BONIFACE. (*Walks slowly towards* ANGELIQUE.) You!
— You were caught with Cot, were you?

ANGELIQUE. (*Crosses Down Right of sofa and runs up
Left Center.*) Merciful Heaven! He thinks it's true!—
He believes it! (*To* BONIFACE, *who follows her below
sofa to Center.*) No, no, no, I tell you! (*Moves forward.*)

BONIFACE. Stand back there! (*He takes her hand and
throws her before him.*)

ANGELIQUE. (*Retreats.*) Benedict!

BONIFACE. (*Moves toward* ANGELIQUE; *furious.*) And
what, may I ask, were you doing with this M. Cot?—
Eh?— What were you *doing?*

ANGELIQUE. (*Up to* BONIFACE.) Nothing—nothing, I
promise you— This is madness!

BONIFACE. (*Brandishing the letter.*) Then how do you
explain this letter? This letter is official! (*Dramatically.*)
What were you doing?— Answer me! (*He grasps her
wrists.*)

ANGELIQUE. Benedict! You're hurting me—you're
hurting me terribly!

BONIFACE. (*Brandishing the boot.*) Take this!

ANGELIQUE. (*Falling on her knees.*) Ah!

VICTOIRE. (*Entering; to Down Left.*) Did you ring,
Monsieur?

BONIFACE. (*Calmly.*) Oh yes—would you mind sew-
ing a button on this boot?

(VICTOIRE *crosses to* BONIFACE.)
Just there.

VICTOIRE. Yes, Monsieur! (*Aside, as she goes out Up
Left.*) What *are* they up to?

BONIFACE. (*Changing his tone—the terror again.*) You
Lucrezia Borgia, you!— You!— The woman I trusted!—
The woman I believed in!!— I always said, my wife
may be a harpy, a gorgon, a bit of a bore, but at least
she's faithful— And now!— Not even that!— Even at
her age—not even that!

ANGELIQUE. But it's a lie, I tell you, a foul lie!

BONIFACE. So that's why you locked me in!— It's all hideously clear!— So that you could indulge your amorous appetites with Cot—! My best friend!

ANGELIQUE. No, no, never!

BONIFACE. (*Crosses below* ANGELIQUE *to her Left.*) *And* where do you go?— To the Paradiso—a disreputable hotel in the Rue de Provence, of all places!

ANGELIQUE. Never! —Never, I tell you— I didn't even know it *was* in the Rue de Provence— Who told *you* it was in the Rue de Provence?

BONIFACE. It's written here. (*Looking at the letter.*) Oh no, it isn't!

ANGELIQUE. You see?— Benedict!— I swear I'm telling you the truth—everything that happened—the runaway horse—the rotten potatoes—the peasants who rescued me!

BONIFACE. And where do these peasants live?

ANGELIQUE. Well—in their village!

BONIFACE. And where *is* their village?

ANGELIQUE. Oh dear Lord!— I don't know— I was whirled away to— I don't know where—miles away!— I should have asked, I know, but with the shock of it all— I never thought— But wait! Cot!— What about Cot? Since he is named too, perhaps *he* will be able to tell you—to explain—

BONIFACE. Very well!— We shall see! (*Crosses below* ANGELIQUE *and Up to Right of trestle table; looking out of the window.*) There he is, crossing the garden! (*Calling.*) Cot! Cot!

COT. (*Off-stage.*) What is it?

BONIFACE. (*Severely.*) Come up here a moment! I have something to say to you!

COT. (*Off-stage.*) What about?

BONIFACE. Come here, and you'll know soon enough!

ANGELIQUE. (*Hands to heaven.*) Oh, you Spirits Above —who know the Unsullied Truth, look down and justify me before This Man!

BONIFACE. (*Bangs trestle table with T-square.*) And

you, Madame, when your accomplice arrives, not a word,
do you understand? Not a gesture!

(ANGELIQUE *crosses to Down Right of sofa.*)
No interruptions during the interrogation!

COT. (*Entering Up Left, to Down Left.*) Well, what
is it?

BONIFACE. (*Center; dignified.*) Stand forward, Monsieur!

COT. (*Astonished, laughing.*) "Stand forward?"—
What on earth's the matter with you?

ANGELIQUE. Ah!— M. Cot!

BONIFACE. Silence, Madame!— Justice must take its
course! (*To* COT.) Where did you say you spent last
night?

COT. At the Hotel Paradiso.

BONIFACE. (*Step Right; triumphant.*) Aha! You hear
that, Madame?

ANGELIQUE. I am going out of my mind!— (*Moves to
below sofa.*) Can it be true that I— Oh! No, no!— It
can't be!— It can't *be?* (*Over to desk.*)

COT. (*Aside.*) What is the matter with them?

BONIFACE. (*Towards* COT.) And who were you *with* at
the Hotel Paradiso, eh? Who were you *with?*

COT. I was alone!

BONIFACE. Come now, Cot, the truth! (*The terror.*)
You were there with Mme. Boniface!

COT. Mme. Boni—!!! What!

BONIFACE. Cot, I know all!— You are my wife's lover!

COT. *Me?*

ANGELIQUE. (*Over to Right end of sofa.*) There, you
see!

BONIFACE. Silence, Madame!

COT. Now what *is* all this? It's a joke!— You're pulling my leg!

BONIFACE. A joke? Aha! Read that! (*He gives him
the summons.*)

COT. (*Reading; crosses below* BONIFACE *to Right Center.*) "To Mme. Boniface, who was caught last night in

a police round-up at the Hotel Paradiso with M. Cot."
(*Laughing.*) Ah— Oh, that's funny!— That's the
funniest thing I ever heard!— But it's a farce!— A practical joke!

BONIFACE. Do I look as if I'm joking?

ANGELIQUE. (*Scarcely able to speak; sits Right end
sofa.*) Yes!— My husband believes that I am capable
of—with *you!* (*Collapses against Right end of sofa.*)

COT. What?— *Me?*—your lover?? (*Trying to suppress
his laughter.*) What a very peculiar idea!

BONIFACE. This is no time for laughter, sir!

COT. You can't be serious! Ah! No, really!— *Me,* the
lover of— (*Lowers voice; cross to Right of* BONIFACE.)
Now look here, old chap, I don't want to be ungracious,
but seriously, before you accuse me— I beg of you, just
have a look at the lady in question— Just have a look
at her!

BONIFACE. Oh, no!— This is no time to start insulting my wife! (*Crosses below* COT *to Center.*)

ANGELIQUE. (*Head on hand.*) He's insulting me?

BONIFACE. (*Indignantly.*) Yes, Madame, that's what
he's doing now!— Desecrating the idol he once wor-
shipped! Casting you in the ashcan like an old squeezed
lemon!

COT. (*Toward* BONIFACE.) No, really! You are being
too absurd!

BONIFACE. How do I know?— Some madman's idea of
a joke, I suppose— And I'll prove it!— If I am im-
plicated in this so-called round-up, how do you explain
the fact that I have received no summons myself—not a
word, do you understand? Nothing! And until such time
as I receive a similar summons, I shall deny everything—

    (VICTOIRE *enters.*)

everything!— To the last ditch!

VICTOIRE. (*To Left of* COT.) A letter for M. Cot from
the Inspector of Police!

      (COT *takes paper.*)

BONIFACE. (*Center; triumphantly.*) Aha!

COT. (*Reading in a low voice.*) "To M. Cot, caught last night in a police round-up at the Hotel Paradiso with *Mme. Boniface!*"

ANGELIQUE. (*Rises and to Right end of sofa.*) No! No!

BONIFACE. That cuts the ground from under your feet, eh? (*Down Center.*)

COT. (*Horrified.*) No, this is the limit!

(*He moves over to* ANGELIQUE; BONIFACE *moves Up Center.*)

ANGELIQUE. I tell you, we are being hounded by Fate!

BONIFACE. (*Crosses Up Center.*) Now do you deny it?— *Do you deny it?*

(COT *and* ANGELIQUE *to Right of commode.*)

COT. (*Dumbfounded.*) I don't understand— I must be going out of my mind!

(*He and* ANGELIQUE *study the papers.*)

VICTOIRE. (*Up to Left of* BONIFACE; *giving him his boot.*) Your boot, Monsieur!

BONIFACE. Thank you *so* much! (*To* COT.) Oh, treachery!

(*Bangs boot on floor;* ANGELIQUE *and* COT *turn;* VICTOIRE *starts for door.*)

Double-dyed treachery!

VICTOIRE. (*Coming back to* BONIFACE.) Beg your pardon, Monsieur?

BONIFACE. I wasn't speaking to you! Be off! (*Hits tray with shoe; puts boot on desk Up Left.*)

VICTOIRE. (*Curtsey.*) Very good, Monsieur! (*She goes out Up Left.*)

COT. (*Seeing* MARCELLE *come in to Down Left.*) Marcelle!

BONIFACE. Oh, it's you, Madame! You're just in time! (*Pointing to* COT.) You see this man?

MARCELLE. (*Astonished.*) My husband?

BONIFACE. (*With eclat.*) Well, he's my wife's lover!

MARCELLE. He *is?*

ANGELIQUE. (*Moves Right; hand to head.*) Merciful Heaven!

(COT *and* ANGELIQUE *up to commode;* ANGELIQUE *Right of* COT.)

BONIFACE. (*Over to Right of* MARCELLE. *In undertone, to* MARCELLE.) It's not true! Faint dead away in my arms!

MARCELLE. Right! (*Falls into his arms.*) A-a-ah!

ANGELIQUE. Look!— Look!

COT. (*Over to Right of* MARCELLE.) It's a lie, I tell you!— A lie!— Oh, Lord!— Marcelle! Marcelle! (*He pats her hands.*) Smelling salts, quickly! Smelling salts!

ANGELIQUE. Wait! I have some in there! (*She exits Left.*)

COT. Smelling salts! Smelling salts! (*He follows* ANGELIQUE *off.*)

MARCELLE. (*Lifting up her head, in undertone.*) What's going on?

BONIFACE. (*Whispering, fast.*) They've received the summons!

MARCELLE. (*Same manner.*) Ah! I get it!

BONIFACE. (*Whispering, faster.*) Look out! Quick! Faint! Faint!

(MARCELLE'S *head falls back on* BONIFACE'S *shoulder.*)

COT. (*Entering, holding smelling salts; crosses below* MARCELLE *to Right of her.* ANGELIQUE *follows him on.*) Here are the salts! (*Pointing the bottle at* BONIFACE *as if it were a revolver.*) What you have just done is an action utterly unworthy of a gentleman!

BONIFACE. You are in no position, sir, to take on airs with me! (*Change of tone.*) Don't push those smelling salts under my nose like that! (*He snatches the bottle.*)

COT. (*Moving away.*) Oh, what a *tragedy!*— A *tragedy!* Water!— Water! (COT *to below commode.*)

ANGELIQUE. Over there! (*Crosses below* MARCELLE *to Left of commode.*)

BONIFACE. (*Undertone, to* MARCELLE.) All right, that'll do! Come to!

MARCELLE. Right ho! (*Coming to.*) Ah!

ANGELIQUE. (*Going Center.*) Look!— She's coming round!

COT. (*To above sofa; to* MARCELLE.) Marcelle! Marcelle! I beg of you!— Don't believe a word he says!

(MARCELLE *and* BONIFACE *rise;* MARCELLE *to Down Left.*)

ANGELIQUE. Yes! It's lies—all lies!

BONIFACE. (*Crossing toward* ANGELIQUE.) I tell you they were both caught together last night, in a police raid. (*Crosses back to* MARCELLE; *undertone.*) Make a scene! Make a scene!

MARCELLE. (*Undertone.*) Right! (*To* COT, *bellowing.*) A-a-a-ah! (*Runs to above sofa.*)

ANGELIQUE. (*Retreats to Up Left Center.*) Heavens above!

COT. Marcelle, I beg of you— I tell you it's a trick, a joke—an odious joke!

MARCELLE. Don't you dare *speak* to me! (*Inspiration.*) So *that* was your so-called ghost! (*Moves to steps and points to* ANGELIQUE.)

BONIFACE. (*Up to Right of* MARCELLE.) Exactly! For him it was a ghost, and for her—a runaway horse!—

(ANGELIQUE *moves to Down Left.*)

And then both return to their homes with identical black eyes!— Like a couple of poached eggs!

MARCELLE. Ha!

COT. (*At Right end of sofa.*) No, really! I've had about enough of this!— So you're both convinced that we were arrested in a police raid last night?

BONIFACE *and* MARCELLE. Yes! We are convinced!

COT. You are? Right! Well then, the four of us will go straight to the Police Inspector, and see if he recognizes us!

VICTOIRE. (*Entering; to Down Left.*) M. Martin!

ALL. M. Martin!

(MARCELLE *to Down Right;* COT *to high-stool;* AN-GELIQUE *to desk Up Left, sits;* BONIFACE *to Center.* VICTOIRE *exits.*)

MARTIN. (*Enters, to Down Left Center.*) Ah! What a night, my friends!— What a *night!* Good *morning,* Boniface!

BONIFACE. (*Over to* MARTIN, *putting his hands on* MARTIN'S *shoulders and pushing him.*) *Would* you mind waiting in my bedroom? (*Pushes* MARTIN *toward Up Right Center.*) We're discussing business!

MARTIN. (*Being pushed.*) Oh! All right!— All right! Good morning, Mme. Cot!— (*Stops and turns.*) Good morning, Mme. Boniface! Oh! Whatever have you done to your eye?

ANGELIQUE. (*Moves Down Left and turns.*) Oh, nothing! Nothing at all!

MARTIN. (*Being pushed back, stops suddenly.*) Do you know what happened to me after I left you last night?

BONIFACE. (*Left of* MARTIN, *pushing him.*) Yes, yes, yes! You can tell me all about it later!

MARTIN. I spent the whole night, with my daughters, at the station!

BONIFACE. (*Quickly.*) At the Railway Station! (*Turning to the others.*) He has great difficulty with his speech!

MARTIN. What *do* you mean—difficulty with my speech!— No such thing!—

BONIFACE. (*Breaks Left and Up Center. At his wits end, aside.*) Oh, if only it would *rain!*

MARTIN. (*Escaping* BONIFACE *and crossing below him to* ANGELIQUE.) Luckily, this morning they found out who we were, and set us free!

BONIFACE. (*Running after him; takes* MARTIN *and pushes him toward bedroom Left.*) Well, now, off you go to my bedroom!— This way!— This way! (*He propels him along.*)

MARTIN. Oh, I've had enough of Paris— I'm going right back to Valence!

BONIFACE. (*Pushing* MARTIN.) You are?— Well then —that way!— That way! (*He turns* MARTIN *sharply around and propels him towards the door Right.*)

MARTIN. No, no, no!— Not just yet!

BONIFACE. Oh!— Well, then, as you were!— This way! This way! Off you go! (*Pushes him into the bedroom Right and returns to Right end of sofa and leans.*)

COT. That man's a nuisance!

MARTIN. (*Opening bedroom door and re-entering to above Center of sofa.*) Oh, by the way, how did *you* two make out last night?

BONIFACE. (*Rushing at him again.*) Oh, splendidly!— Splendidly, thank you! (*Runs above sofa and pushes* MARTIN *towards bedroom.*) Yes. Off you go! Off you go! (*He pushes* MARTIN *into the bedroom and shuts the door.*)

ANGELIQUE. (*Moves toward Center; to her husband.*) What did he mean, "How did *you* make out last night?"

BONIFACE. (*At Right end of sofa.*) Oh, nothing! Nothing!— It's a well-known expression in the provinces. Whenever they want to ask someone if they slept well, they say, "How did you make out last night?"

ANGELIQUE. Ah!— Well, I never knew that! (*Steps Left.*)

COT. (*Rises and down to Left of* MARCELLE.) Well now, come along, everybody— Off we go to Headquarters to see the Inspector of Police!

(BONIFACE *runs to sofa; sits Left end.* ANGELIQUE *pulls* BONIFACE *towards Left;* COT *pulls* MARCELLE *towards Left.*)

BONIFACE *and* MARCELLE. No! No!

VICTOIRE. (VICTOIRE *enters Up Left. Announcing.*) The Inspector of Police!

ALL. The Inspector of Police!

BONIFACE. He can't come in!

COT. But he's just in time! (*Turns to* MARCELLE.)

BONIFACE. (*Aside.*) We're ditched! (*Moves up to high stool and sits.*)

(MARCELLE *sits chair Down Right.* INSPECTOR OF POLICE *enters.* BONIFACE *turns his back on him.*)

COT *and* ANGELIQUE. Come in, Monsieur! Come right in!

(COT *over to Left of door Up Left.*)

INSPECTOR. M. Cot, if you please! I wish to speak to M. Cot!

ANGELIQUE. You mean *us,* Inspector! Here we are!

COT. Here I am, Monsieur! At your service! (*He precedes* INSPECTOR *downstage.*)

INSPECTOR. Oh, I'm sorry, Monsieur, I didn't recognize you right away. Of course when I saw you last night, your face was smeared with some black concoction!

COT. *Mine* was?

INSPECTOR. But now, of course, I can recognize you perfectly!

COT *and* ANGELIQUE. What?

BONIFACE. (*Undertone, to* MARCELLE.) He recognizes him!

COT. You say you recognize me?

INSPECTOR. Oh, naturally! After all, I was the one who caught you with Mme. Boniface last night, at the Hotel Paradiso!

ANGELIQUE. Me? *Me?*— You caught *me?*

INSPECTOR. (*Turning towards* ANGELIQUE.) Ah! Mme. Boniface, I presume!

ANGELIQUE. (*Faces front.*) Yes, Inspector, I am Mme. Boniface!

INSPECTOR. You must forgive me, Madame. It was so difficult to see your face clearly last night under that lace scarf!

ANGELIQUE. My face?

INSPECTOR. But now, of course, I remember you very well!

COT *and* ANGELIQUE. What?

BONIFACE. Now he remembers *her!*

ANGELIQUE. You say you remember me?

COT. But, Inspector, you can't possibly remember us— for the very good reason that you never *did* arrest us at this Hotel Paradiso!

INSPECTOR. What do you mean, I never arrested you! Why, I questioned you in detail, and released you on bail!

COT. If you arrested anyone, they must have been impostors who took on our names and identities!

INSPECTOR. (*Unbelieving.*) Yes, yes, of course. But anyway, don't let that worry you, it's not at all important!

COT *and* ANGELIQUE. What do you mean?— Not important?

INSPECTOR. When I found out who you were, I was extremely sorry that my secretary had sent you that summons. To you, of all people, to *the* M. Cot, the President of The Builders Association. Why, you're just the man I'm looking for! I badly need an expert, and I didn't know who to go to!

Cot. But, Inspector—

INSPECTOR. Yes, sir! I am delighted to make your acquaintance—you see, it's like this: I have a charming little house in the country—

Cot. (*Breaking to below* ANGELIQUE *and* INSPECTOR *to Up Left.*) I don't give a damn about your little house in the country!— It's this lady and gentleman I'm concerned about! (*He indicates* BONIFACE *and* MARCELLE.)

INSPECTOR. (*Bowing.*) How do you do, Monsieur?—
   (BONIFACE *rises to Right of stool, bows to* IN-
   SPECTOR.)

My respects, Madame!

(MARCELLE *rises and* INSPECTOR *and* MARCELLE *bow.*
MARCELLE *sits.*)

Cot. Thanks to your summons, our respective spouses are still under the impression that—well, anyway, as the whole thing is a pack of lies, I insist that you did *not* arrest the two of us.

INSPECTOR. Aha! Well, M'sieu, that *is* a little difficult for me!

Cot. Well, for heaven's sake try to remember! Think carefully! Look well at both of us! (*Steps Left.*)

ANGELIQUE. Even if you didn't see the lady's face, surely you remember her figure—her silhouette— (*Crosses Down Left and pirouettes, hand in air.*)

(BONIFACE *hurriedly hides* MARCELLE *from the* INSPEC-
TOR'S *eye.*)

INSPECTOR. (*Moves toward* Cot.) Well!— As to that —it did seem to me that the lady wasn't quite so—er— that she was of rather less—er—ambitious proportions!—
   (BONIFACE *sneaks down to above* MARCELLE.)

But that could be an optical illusion!— After all, my

office is large, with a high ceiling, so naturally that rather alters the scale of things!

ANGELIQUE. Impertinence!

INSPECTOR. There's one thing I do remember, though. (*General alert.*)

The lady in question wore a mauve dress.

ANGELIQUE. That settles it! I don't possess one!

MARCELLE. (*Rises briskly.*) Neither do I!

BONIFACE. (*Hits* MARCELLE *on head with quill and throws it on desk.*) Don't do that!

(MARCELLE *sits.*)

COT. (*To* MARCELLE.) Eh? But *you* don't come into this! (*Two steps Up.*)

INSPECTOR. (*To* ANGELIQUE.) But, unfortunately, all that is too vague to allow for any uncertainty as to your identity.

COT. Now listen, you must have arrested some other people as well as us last night— Isn't that so? Well, then, why don't you question them? See if they recognize us or not! Who were these people?

INSPECTOR. (*Upstage to* COT.) Wait! I have the list here!

COT. Give it to me! (*Reading.*) Bonnard, the Bull of the Bistros!— Don't know him!— Adele Dubois, known as the Tiger Lily!— Hector Mush, alias Florizei— M. Martin and his four daughters— (*Quickly.*) Martin— Which Martin?— Surely there is a M. Martin here in the house!

BONIFACE. (*Aside.*) Damnation!

INSPECTOR. Here?

ANGELIQUE. Yes! And he has four daughters!

COT. And, what's more, he told us that he'd just spent the night at the Station!

BONIFACE. (*Quickly.*) At the Railway Station!

COT. No, no! You said the Railway Station— He just said the Station!

INSPECTOR. Well, he must be our man!

ANGELIQUE. (*Crosses above* COT *and* INSPECTOR *into bedroom Right.*) Aha! Well, now we shall see! Let's ask him right away. (*Calling.*) Mr. Martin! Mr. Martin!

(COT *follows her off.*)

MARCELLE. (*Undertone, to* BONIFACE.) Boniface— I feel myself sinking—sinking into the bowels of the earth!

BONIFACE. (*Pushing* MARCELLE *into chair Down Right.*) Oh, don't do that!

COT. (*Pushing* MARTIN *in to Right of* BONIFACE.) Mr. Martin! Mr. Martin! Come right in! Right this way, sir!

(ANGELIQUE *enters and stays by door.*)

MARTIN. What is it?— What is it? (*Seeing* INSPECTOR.) The Police Inspector! Oh, I can't stand that again!

(*Runs to bedroom,* COT *runs and stops him;* ANGELIQUE, COT *and* MARTIN *come Center.*)

COT. Mr. Martin, you are the only one to save us from an impossible situation!

ANGELIQUE. I beg of you! Tell them the truth! You alone can save us!

INSPECTOR. Mr. Martin, try to remember everything that occurred!

MARTIN. Please! *Please!* Mesdames! Messieurs! Don't all speak at the same time— I can't make head or tail of what you're saying!

COT. M. Martin, you were at the Hotel Paradiso last night, were you not?

MARTIN. Not only was I there, but I was arrested— I can't imagine why— I shall never forget it!

COT. But tell me, did you see *us* there? I mean Mme. Boniface and myself?

MARTIN. Me?— No, I didn't see you!

ANGELIQUE. (*To* INSPECTOR.) You see?

MARTIN. When I think of how my poor little girls were dragged off to the Police Station with me, and had to spend the whole night there!—

COT. Yes. If you didn't see us, were there other people that you *did* see?

(BONIFACE *moves below and to Left of* MARCELLE.)

MARTIN. Other people?— Of course there were other people!

INSPECTOR, COT *and* ANGELIQUE. (*Quickly.*) Well, who?— Who?

MARTIN. Well, that's very easy to answer!

(BONIFACE *moves front of sofa;* MARCELLE *rises.*)

BONIFACE *and* MARCELLE. This is it!

MARTIN. (*To* BONIFACE, *laughing.*) Do you hear that, Boniface? They want to know whom I saw last night!

BONIFACE. (*With a forced laugh.*) Yes!— I heard! I heard! (*Crosses and sits Center of sofa.*)

MARTIN. (*Crosses Down above sofa.*) You want to know who I saw?

(BONIFACE *tugs at the bottom of* MARTIN's *coat.*) What are you doing to my coat? (*Back up. To* AN-GELIQUE.) Well, I saw—

(*Sound of a crash of* THUNDER *followed by hail on the window panes.*)

—the bi—er—er—the bi—de—

ANGELIQUE. What's the matter with you?

MARCELLE. (*Aside.*) He's stuttering!

BONIFACE. (*Standing upon a chair, his arms raised in joy to heaven.*) It's the rain!— Praise be on high!

INSPECTOR. (*To* MARTIN.) Well, Monsieur, come along! Answer!— Who did you see?

MARTIN. Er—er— Yes—the bede—er— Para— Para

— Paradiso— Ho— Ho— Ho— (*He kicks out.*) er—
er—er! Oh, pish! (*Up to top of steps.*)

BONIFACE. He's never stuttered better!

ANGELIQUE. M. Martin, you are doing this on purpose!
Speak up!

MARTIN. The bede—bede—bede— Yes!

COT. We'll never get anything out of him!

INSPECTOR. (*Sudden inspiration.*) Wait! I know the
solution.

(RAIN *fades out.*)

ALL. What!

INSPECTOR. He must commit his evidence to writing!

COT *and* ANGELIQUE. (*To front and then to each
other.*) Yes, yes, of course!

(BONIFACE *hisses.*)

MARTIN. Yes!

INSPECTOR. (*To* MARTIN.) Here you are, my good sir,
just sit yourself down here

    (COT *takes* MARTIN *down Right to desk.*)

and write down exactly who you saw last night. (*He
makes to get paper and pen.*)

MARCELLE. (*Aside to* BONIFACE.) Ah! Now it's out!

(BONIFACE *leads* MARCELLE *above sofa to Up Left.*)

BONIFACE. (*Aside.*) We're lost!

COT, INSPECTOR *and* ANGELIQUE. (*All making signs to*
MARTIN.) Go on!— Go on! Write! Write! Write!

MAXIME. (MAXIME *enters Up Left with his hat in his
hand.*) Oh!— Quite a gathering! (*Aside.*) Lord!—there's
that man from the hotel last night! (*He hides his face
with his hat.*) If he sees me, everything will come out!
(*Crosses Up Right and then Up Center. He sees the
blackened napkin that* BONIFACE *has used to wipe his*

face.) Oh! (*He puts the napkin over his head and then puts his hat on, and tries to climb over the window-sill.*)

MARTIN. (*Pointing out* MAXIME *to* COT *and* MRS. BONIFACE.) The Bo!— The Bo!

BONIFACE. (*Seeing* MAXIME, *crying out.*) Ah! Stop thief!

ALL. Whatever is that?

(COT *runs to the window.*)

INSPECTOR. (*Following.*) Wait!— This is my business!
(COT *takes* MAXIME *by one arm, and* INSPECTOR *by the other.*)
(*Trying to snatch off the napkin.*) Monsieur! In the name of the law—

MAXIME. (*Struggling.*) Let me go!— Let me go!

INSPECTOR *and* COT. Will you take it off!— Will you take it *off?*

MAXIME. No! No! No!

(COT *pulls off the napkin.*)

ALL. (*Point.*) Maxime!

INSPECTOR. Aha! The man! Last night!

ALL. What!

INSPECTOR. The black face! There he is!

ALL. (*Toward front.*) Maxime!

COT. You miserable wretch— It was *you?*

MAXIME. What d'you mean me? What's the matter with them?

INSPECTOR. It was you, Monsieur! You were in the Hotel Paradiso last night?

MAXIME. What? Oh, so you know about it!

ALL. (*Point.*) It was him!

BONIFACE. (*To* INSPECTOR.) You hear? He admits it! He admits it!

MARTIN. (*Moving Down below* BONIFACE.) But er— er—er!

BONIFACE. (*Grabs* MARTIN *and puts him back in place.*) Yes, yes! Be quiet, you!

ANGELIQUE. Who were you with? You don't dare to suggest that you were with me?

MAXIME. (*Comes Center.*) With *you?*— Good Lord!— I should say *not!*

INSPECTOR. With whom, then?— You *were* with a woman!

ALL. Yes! Whom were you with?

MAXIME. (*To front.*) Oh well! Here goes!— (*To four at Left.*) with Victoire.

ALL. Victoire!

COT. Well, where is she?— Where is this woman? (*Crosses below past* MME. BONIFACE.)

ANGELIQUE. She's in her room—

COT. In her room! One moment! (*Runs to door Up Left. Calling.*) Victoire! Victoire!

MARTIN. (*Starts toward door.*) Wa—wa—wa—wait!

BONIFACE. (*Pulls* MARTIN *to desk Up Left; giving him a hefty push.*) Yes, yes! Be quiet, you!— Leave us alone!

(MARTIN *goes to the desk to write his evidence.*)

COT. (*Now off-stage.*) Victoire— Come down here this instant!

VICTOIRE. (*Off-stage.*) But I haven't finished dressing yet, Monsieur!

(COT *re-enters, followed by* VICTOIRE.)

COT. (*Crosses to chair Down Right and pulls it out.*) Never mind about finishing dressing— *Will* you come *here* at once!

(EVERYONE *comes downstage except* MARTIN, *who stays up at the desk, writing.*)

ALL. (*Pointing.*) The mauve dress!

(VICTOIRE *twirls toward Right in front of line-up.*)

ANGELIQUE. Where did you get that dress?

VICTOIRE. (*Below Center of sofa.*) It's a dress I was just trying on— It was given to me!

BONIFACE. Yes, yes! No need to explain! No need to explain!

COT. You admit that you spent last night at the Hotel Paradiso?

VICTOIRE. What? (*To line-up.*) Oh, so you know about it?

ANGELIQUE. And you had the audacity to use my name?

VICTOIRE. *Me?*

BONIFACE. Yes!— No need to explain!— No need to explain! (*Step to Right end of sofa.*) Be off!— You must leave this house instantly! (*He pushes her towards the door Up Left.*)

ANGELIQUE. (*Comes down.*) But—my dear—really!—

BONIFACE. (*Holding her back.*) Don't implicate your-self!— Don't *implicate* yourself! (*To* VICTOIRE.) Now, you heard what I said— Off with you! Bag and baggage! This very instant! (*Follows* VICTOIRE *to Up Left; pushes her off.*)

VICTOIRE. (*As she disappears.*) Lord save us! They've all gone berserk! (*Exit* VICTOIRE.)

BONIFACE. Well now!— That's that! (*At door.*)

MARTIN. (*Who has finished writing his evidence, to* INSPECTOR.) Here's my evi— evi— evi— evi—

BONIFACE. (*Quickly.*) Eh—what's that?— Your evi-dence? Good gracious me, we've no need of all that *now!*— (*Walks below line-up to Down Center.*) We know all the facts— We've no need of *that* any more!

(COT *crosses up above line-up into* BONIFACE'S *place.*)

ALL. No! No! No! We don't need it any more!

(BONIFACE *tears up* MARTIN'S *deposition and throws the pieces in the air.*)

MARTIN. Oh!

BONIFACE. (*Looking at his watch.*) By Jove! You've just got time to catch your train! Off you go!— Back to Valence!

ALL. (*Pushing* MARTIN *towards the door.*) Yes, yes, yes!— Back, back, back to Valence!

MARTIN. Bu—bu—bu—bu—bu——but it's ra—ra— (*Kick.*) raining!

BONIFACE. Oh, but it's lovely (*Kick.*) in Valence! Off you go!

ALL. Yes, off to Valence! It's gorgeous in Valence!

(MARTIN *is whirled off by* ALL.)

INSPECTOR. (*Crosses to Down Right of sofa;* MAXIME *follows.*) And now, young man, since the whole incident is closed, allow me to return the twenty thousand francs that belong to you!

MAXIME. To *me?*

BONIFACE. (*Enters and up to high stool. Aside.*) A-a-a-ah! My twenty thousand francs!

MAXIME. How do you mean, they belong to *me?*

INSPECTOR. Well, naturally they do, since you were the man in the Hotel Paradiso!

ALL. Bravo!

MAXIME. So they give you a bonus!

BONIFACE. (*To the audience.*) It's a disaster! I've kept me virtue *and* lost me francs! (*Runs Down and jumps onto sofa.*)

MAXIME. (*Sitting.*) What a happy ending!

BONIFACE. What a hotel!

ALL. (*With a great gesture.*) What a *night!!* What a *night!!* (*To front.*)

CURTAIN

PROPERTY PLOT

ACT ONE

Hand Props and Dressings

Plans and blueprints (clipped to wall either side window (UC)
In rack (DS of desk DR)
Rolls of architects drawings and French newspapers
On desk (DR)
Blotter, plan, ink stand, letter rack, 2 books, 1 T-square, pencil, quill, 3 statuettes, pewter box, candlestick, small urn w/flowers
On commode (R of steps C)
Serviette (blackened, preset Act III), Brown vase w/flowers, sphynx, gold statuette w/candelabra, sea shell crockery, double photo frame, 2 large books, gold turtle on oak leaf, gold inlaid urn
On sofa (DRC)
Leopard skin (back of sofa should be 1 notch down from upright position)
On trestle table (UC)
Box drawing instr., plan, 2 rulers, T-square, triangle, 2 white quills, 4 books, masonry brick, grey quill
On floor by trestle table
(Near DL leg) French telephone book (leaning against leg), 2 plans, grey quill (behind leg) (near DR leg) Builders Tile (between legs)
On desk (US of UL door)
Penknife, writing paper (One blank on top of Martin's evidence, preset for Act III), ink set w/quill, photo frame in top right sec. of desk w/*Bon. bowler hat set on it. Plan w/backing rolled (on ink set)*, pencil, ink jar, small vase w/flowers, large china bust, vase w/cat-o-nine-tails.

124

Fire box (*below window C*)

(This box fastened securely to stage floor), rope ladder (in box fastened to stage), fire ax (fastened to closed side of top)

Key in Door Lock UL

Off Right

Personal props given to Boniface before each performance: French coins -3-, pencil, key, tape measure

Off Left

Props held by actors, checked before each performance: cigar—Cot, handkerchief—Marcelle, book and pince nez—Max, hat, hatpin, brown jacket—Angelique

(*On Prop table*)

French coins—(Martin), umbrella—(Martin), 2 lengths of materials (yellow and red)—(Angelique), small card tray w/calling card—(Victoire), *large silver tray:*—(Victoire), (*on this:*) Sister's letter, dressmaker's bill, 3 Paradiso circulars

Dinner tray: (Victoire)

(*on this:*) place mat, napkin, knife, fork, spoon, china plate w/silver cover, water glass, water jug (½ filled)

Door bolt (behind door UL)

5 trunks

FURNITURE

Music rack (DS of desk DR), desk (DR), Mirror (above desk DR), plants (in pots L and R of window C), side chair (on st. desk DR—shoved in), small ottoman (US desk DR), Commode (R of steps C), sofa (DRC), trestle table (UC in alcove), high stool (DS of trestle), pot plant on ped. (DS of desk DR), fire box (below window UC), side chair (at desk UL), pot. plant in tall vase (betw. 2 doors SL), side chair (DL), drapes (archway to alcove), parquet ground cloth, rug (C of set), 2 framed Chinese Paintings (above desk UL)

ACT TWO

HAND PROPS AND DRESSINGS

On mantel (bedroom No. 10)
Water pitcher (filled), water glass, clock, pr. candelabra,
ashtray (water in this)
In fireplace
Pr. firedogs
On hallway desk
Drill (in drawer), box of matches (in drawer), ledger
and pencil, 6 candlesticks (elec.) (US one lit at rise), 2
LG candles (precut halfway through to break in half),
No. 10 key on keyboard, hall (all keys nailed down ex-
cept No. 10)
In bedroom No. 11
Ashtray w/matchholder on table C and matches in holder
Off Left
(Top of stairs) hand bell, stone hot water bottle, (under
backstage escape stairs on platform landing) trick hat—
Cot
Off Right
3 side chairs, tray no. 1: kettle, stand with lamp (elec.),
teapot, milk server, 2 cups and saucers w/spoons, tray
No. 2: 5 cups and saucers, sugar bowl (filled w/cubes);
hand bell, dummy police club, cigar and matches (Boniface), traveling case (Boniface)
4 wicker cases:
In each: night lite (elec.), box matches, curling tongs,
stuffing inside to prevent rattling; Gladstone bag (Cot),
in this: comb, 2 brushes, mirror, box of cigars, nightshirt,
slippers; satchel w/strap (Max), school books strapped
together (Victoire), blackening make-up (Boniface)
*(Props being handled by actors and keep same with
them for the run)*
Cheroot (make of wood doweling, 3″ long, painted
brown) (Martin), 4 police whistles, handkerchief (Marcelle)

Furniture

Bedroom No. 10 (Stage Right)
Pedestal table 2/red bobble table cover, straight back chair (breakaway), bed (UL) w/covers, small table (DS of bed), mirror (above mantel), wall brackets (each side of mirror), floor carpet

Bedroom No. 11 (Stage Left)
Table (C), 4 single iron beds w/coverlets), 2 side chairs (1 bet. L. Pr. beds, 1 UR of alcove), bed (built into alcove), draperies, red (alcove), small table, pedestal (UL), carpeting.

Hall (Stage Center)
Nos. 9, 10, 11 (door plates), table with drawer, side chair, key rack w/hooks and keys (all nailed down except No. 10), parquet ground cloth, stair runner (red)

ACT THREE

Hand Props and Dressings

The onstage props and furniture are exactly the same as at the end of Act I. The rope ladder is still hanging out the window. No one has been in the room since the end of Act I. The following is the additions and alterations made for the playing of the act:

Dinner tray (on trestle table)
Napkin (is changed for towel cut to same size and a blob of cleansing grease in its center), plan w/backing (put on trestle), grey quill (on plan), T-square on trestle (must be free and clear), key (by DL leg of sofa)

Off Right
Smoking jacket (Boniface), single boot (Boniface) (on chair near DR door)

Off Left
Telegram (Victoire)

On tray
2 police notices (both in envelopes), 1 addressed to Cot,

1 addressed to Mme. Boniface (Victoria carries each on separately), smelling salts bottle

Personal Props held by actors for run

Cigarette in holder (Max), roll of 20,000 franc notes (Inspector), notebook and pencil, rain effects (props), chimes (props)

COSTUME PLOT

(*Period 1910*)

BONIFACE: *Act One:* Black cut-away coat—white handkerchief, blue (light) vest, checked trousers, black string bow tie, black high-button shoes w. gray tops, white shirt w. detached collar, black derby (or "shovel" hat)—this preset on stage. *Act Two:* Same. *Act Three:* Same plus wine colored velvet smoking jacket, brocade house slippers.

MME. BONIFACE: *Act One:* Mustard wool "Princess"; black lace yoke, neck and sleeves, matching Dolman fingertip length coat, black velvet draw-string handbag, black gloves, black shoes and stockings—black slip or petticoat, black straw and fruit decoration on top (hat). *Act Three:* Same plus change of hat (Act III hat is copy of Act I hat, in very bad condition), wig—dressed high on head.

MARCELLE: *Act One:* Blonde wig, pink silk negligee w. pink feather trim, pink slip, pink satin-covered slippers w/pompoms, white chiffon handkerchief; change into dark red 2-piece suit (Bolero jacket), pink net and lace ruffled blouse, stockings to go with both negligee and this dress, bronze leather slippers w. straps, red velvet belt w. silver buckle, pink full petticoat. *Act Two:* Mauve dress, mauve petticoat, light pink lace scarf, "Opera length" light beige gloves, purple shoes w. strap, light-colored leghorn hat (trim: red roses and black ribbon). *Act Three:* Same as 2nd Act I outfit *minus* bolero jacket.

MAXIME: *Act One:* Blonde wig, light gray tweed suit

(lower back slit and flared out), black high-button shoes w. gray tops, white shirt w. high stiff collar, light blue narrow necktie—fancy flowered vest, pince nez, black socks, suspenders. *Acts Two and Three:* Same plus "Boater" hat.

M. Cot: *Act One:* Red wig, beard and moustache, olive gray cut-away coat and trousers w. black trim, vest—oyster white w. green buttons, black high-button shoes w. gray tops, white shirt and stiff collar, Ascot tie w. stickpin, large white handkerchief (in sleeve cuff), watch chain, pince nez (½ lenses) on black ribbon, black socks. *Act Two:* Same as Act I plus tall silk hat (N.B.: extra large special "Prop" hat off at top of stairs for quick change at Act II finale). *Act Three:* Same as Act I.

M. Martin: *Act One:* Donigale tweed cut-away coat and trousers, cream-colored waistcoat, black shoes, white spats, white shirt w. stiff collar, cream-colored satin four-in-hand tie, plaid inverness cape, gray wig, moustache and beard, gray homburg hat, yellow gloves, umbrella, suspenders. *Act Two:* Same as Act I. Change into cotton nightgown and slippers. *Act Three:* Same as Act I *minus* hat and cape and gloves and umbrella.

Victoire: *Act One:* Black wig, black alpaca dress (uniform), white apron w. yoke front and crossed behind back, white cuffs and collar, white maid's cap w. long streamers behind, black stockings, white petticoat, black high-button boots. *Act Two:* Pink-yellow polka dot dress, feather boa, pink hat (lampshade type) with white ribbon, black and white high-button shoes, black stockings, black belt. *Act Three:* Same as Act I; change into exact copy "Marcelle's" Act II mauve dress (continue to wear black stockings and black high-button boots).

Four Daughters: *Act One:* Black semi-high button shoes, black stockings over white stockings, ½ petticoats w. eyelet trim, red velvet coats w. white fur trim, white fur muffs on white silk cords, white cotton gloves, red wide round hats: eyelet trim under brims: pink ribbons around crowns. *Act Two:* Same as Act I, change into long white cotton nightgowns, pink hair ribbon bows (2 per girl), white stockings.

FOUR PORTERS: *Act One:* Blue blouses: below waist length, black trousers—T shirts, black high lace shoes or boots, dark blue caps w. patent leather visors, wide black belts w. buckles, black moustaches and sideburns.

FOUR COPS: *Act Two:* French police hats, navy blue wool jackets, black belts, trousers and boots (same as worn by porters in Act I), black moustaches (these should be different from "Porters").

TABU: *Act Two:* Black trousers, black moustache, Beige "Prince Albert" coat, red Turkish fez w. black tassel, black shoes, white shirt w. stand-up collar, black silk scarf or necktie.

INSPECTOR: *Act Two:* Black and gray wide-striped suit (coat—double breasted), black shoes, black bowler hat, white shirt w. white stiff turn-down collar. *Act Three:* Same as Act II.

ANNIELLO: *Act Two:* Orange wool trousers, red and white candy stripe shirt, gray vest, black string tie, house slippers, black socks, black wig and moustache.

GEORGES: *Act Two:* Black pants, light blue collarless shirt, blue and yellow vest w. black sleeve, black shoes, green wool apron.